CW00970381

G R JORDAN

Implosion

A Kirsten Stewart Thriller #11

You must learn to think one octave higher. Only then will you learn how implosion energy works.

VICTOR SCHAUBERGER

Contents

Foreword

The events of this book, while based around real locations in the north of Scotland, are entirely fictional and all characters do not represent any living or deceased person. All companies are fictitious representations.

Acknowledgement

To Ken, Jean, Colin, Evelyn, John and Rosemary for your work in bringing this novel to completion, your time and effort is deeply appreciated.

Novels by G R Jordan

The Highlands and Islands Detective series (Crime)

1. Water's Edge
2. The Bothy
3. The Horror Weekend
4. The Small Ferry
5. Dead at Third Man
6. The Pirate Club
7. A Personal Agenda
8. A Just Punishment
9. The Numerous Deaths of Santa Claus
10. Our Gated Community
11. The Satchel
12. Culhwch Alpha
13. Fair Market Value
14. The Coach Bomber
15. The Culling at Singing Sands
16. Where Justice Fails
17. The Cortado Club
18. Cleared to Die
19. Man Overboard!
20. Antisocial Behaviour
21. Rogues' Gallery
22. The Death of Macleod - Inferno Book 1

Kirsten Stewart Thrillers (Thriller)

Jac Moonshine Thrillers

3. Jac the Pariah

The Contessa Munroe Mysteries (Cozy Mystery)

1. Corpse Reviver
2. Frostbite
3. Cobra's Fang

The Patrick Smythe Series (Crime)

1. The Disappearance of Russell Hadleigh
2. The Graves of Calgary Bay
3. The Fairy Pools Gathering

Austerley & Kirkgordon Series (Fantasy)

1. Crescendo!
2. The Darkness at Dillingham
3. Dagon's Revenge
4. Ship of Doom

Supernatural and Elder Threat Assessment Agency (SETAA)
Series (Fantasy)

1. Scarlett O'Meara: Beastmaster

Island Adventures Series (Cosy Fantasy Adventure)

1. Surface Tensions

Dark Wen Series (Horror Fantasy)

1. The Blasphemous Welcome
2. The Demon's Chalice

Chapter 01

Dermott Blanwen had stepped off the plane feeling somewhat jaded after the early morning flight. He'd been in London and had stayed the night at a rather inexpensive hotel, catching up with some communications he'd failed to read the day before. Most things were routine, but a visit to London was never good.

Godfrey was a man who wanted all the details, and you never were sure what details he had that you didn't. After all, he wasn't head of the Service for no reason, but Dermott had done well. Recently promoted to take care of the Glasgow operation, it had been joined by Inverness. This made Dermott in charge of them all. Admittedly, there were only eight colleagues, but that was quite large for some departments within the Service.

At thirty-three, Dermott was also ready to take on the world. Young enough to still be fit enough to do the job, he was sharp and had just enough experience to know what he was doing. He must know what he was doing. After all, Godfrey put him in that position. He reported occasionally to Anna Hunt. A more formidable woman he'd never met, but she was also a teacher. Unlike Godfrey, who just expected the results, Anna took time out to coach you, to allow you to develop. She clearly saw that her future was Dermott being the best he could be. His progression was something that would benefit her in the long run.

Dermott had come through arrivals at Glasgow Airport, picked up his car from the long-stay car park, briefly checking it, before getting inside. It was a routine practice for someone in his position, but in truth, there was nothing on the go at the moment. Certainly, nothing that would make him fear for his life. His biggest struggle in the next hour would be the Glasgow traffic. That was the joy of red-eye flights. You got up so early in the morning, then you landed right in the middle of a busy traffic hour wherever you would be.

The operation was run from a quiet street close to the city centre. It was one of the older buildings, and the Service occupied all of it. At the bottom was the recruitment agency, or so it was said to be. But that was just the front door because up above on the other two floors, Dermott ran his operation. They kept tabs on those against the government who raised their heads, intervening when things were beyond the remit of the normal police force.

The traffic into Glasgow was indeed hell, but the day was bright, and Dermott sat listening to the radio as he arrived. He'd become accustomed to the Scottish stations rather than the national ones and thought of this as part of his integration. He was thoroughly English and had graduated from Cambridge University. They picked him up there, seeing his keen brain, and in the year that followed, he was tested many times, starting out as a junior operative. He had spent most of his life in the field and, yes, he'd seen a few things.

Most recent was the chaos in London, the one that had narrowly been averted when someone from outside the agency had stepped in. There were rumours of her banded about his level. Stewart had said she ran the Inverness office at one point, but Anna Hunt was tight-lipped about her. Then again, Anna Hunt was tight-lipped about a lot of things. Oh, yes, she would coach, but if you weren't on a need-to-know basis, you didn't get to know.

As he sat in the queue of traffic, not making any headway into Glasgow City Centre, he thought about his meeting with Godfrey. It had seemed peculiar, for the man had questioned him on a lot of things. If he hadn't known better, or indeed had it been done under other circumstances such as Dermott being strapped to a chair and having a few punches thrown in between the questions, he would have thought it was an interrogation. One of those where you try to find the truth, or you try to rat something out. However, Dermott had seemed to come up to scratch. Godfrey had shaken his hand on the way out. A man not really known for that.

The traffic on the M8 into the city was coming down off the motorway and converging to where some of it slipped into the city centre. Others tried to either pass through on their way up to the north or down to the south, or else make their way across to Edinburgh. Dermott pulled off in towards the city centre, feeling the traffic moving slightly better before he arrived on the street where he worked. He found a space, parked, took his briefcase out from the boot, and walked towards the rather mundane building in front of him.

Yes, everything was good. Godfrey was satisfied. He'd made it through to work on time, and now he would see what his troops were up to. It will be a day at the desk, a day when he didn't have to work that hard. As he took his next step towards the building, less than fifty yards ahead of him, a

3

fierce explosion ripped out from the basement.

Dermott was pushed back, thrown to the floor. He dropped his briefcase and then tried to haul himself up, his ears ringing. There was dust everywhere, and he left the briefcase behind, knowing there was nothing of importance in it. It was just a travelling dummy. Anything of note coming from Godfrey would be kept in his head or sent via secure networks. He wouldn't just carry it around with him.

He turned and sprinted towards the building, his feet crunching on broken glass. As he took the first couple of steps up to the front door, he realised it was gone and, as the dust thinned out, he could see inside. Fire was spreading. He investigated the room on the left where the receptionist sat. Ann, known as his guard dog. There wasn't much of Ann left. He looked towards the back of the room. Sarah would sit there. There was no sign of her.

'Help!' shouted a voice from up above. Dermott looked up. Half of Jane was hanging through a hole in the floor.

'I'm slipping,' she said. 'I'm slipping. You need to—'

'Hold on,' said Dermott. Stepping back outside into the hallway, he saw the stairs were broken. He took the first five, made a leap, clearing another two, and found that the one above was still intact. Continuing up, he felt himself pushed back by a raft of flames. He pulled his jacket over himself and jumped through them.

'Anyone else on the floor?' Dermott shouted. 'Anyone else?'

Jane was hanging out through the hole, and he saw her slip. Desperately, he flung himself forward, grabbing hold of her ankles, and then working his way up her legs before holding her hips. It was a strange angle to approach a woman from but needs must. Pulling her hips back, he pulled her out of the hole in front of her. He turned her over and saw her tattered blouse. Her face was black, and the hair was deeply matted.

'Are you okay?' Dermott asked.

'There's something in my side,' she said. He looked down at a wedge of wood peering out from underneath the blouse. He pulled the blouse up and saw the blood oozing out from the wound.

'Is it all right?' she said.

It isn't, Dermott thought. *It really isn't.* He needed an ambulance. He needed one quick.

'I'm going to get you out of here,' he said. 'Hold on for me.'

He saw eyes of trust looking back at him. Jane was only twenty-five, and Dermott had seen her as a potential companion. The thing about being in the Service was you didn't tell anyone you were with that you were in it. This led to great difficulty. Yet, when he'd arrived in Glasgow and seen Jane with her long, dark hair and smiling face, he had thought to himself that she might be someone he could get close to.

They'd been out a few times. Not on a date, just out to talk. That happened quite a bit in the community. After all, who else did you talk to about any of this? The shrink they provided you? They were as cold as anything.

Then there had been dinner, and then—well, then work had got in the way. London had gone crazy, and by the time all that was resolved, they were both just exhausted. He was hoping to get back on that trail, hoping to get to know her even better, but here she was with a piece of wood sticking out of her.

He helped Jane sit up, and she cried in pain as she did so. The floor across from him was burning up from underneath. A part of it crashed through. There was no time to stay.

'Have you heard of anybody above? Did you hear any cries?'

'Andy shot past me. He's—I think he's gone. Some of the rest were downstairs. I—'

'Shush,' said Dermott. He bent down, grabbed her hips, leaned his shoulder into her, and picked her up over his shoulder. He heard her try to stifle her cry of pain, failing in the main, but it didn't matter. They had to get out of here.

Jane wasn't heavy, and Dermott was reasonably strong. Taking the first couple of steps, he came to the gap in the stairs. He jumped, landing on the first one after the gap. He felt the stair shake and quickly tried to step off the one he was on. It half gave way as he moved, and he stumbled down the rest of the stairs before careering into the brickwork beside the front door. He spun out of that, stumbled down a couple of steps and collapsed, dropping Jane onto the floor.

He looked up; the wind knocked out of him but smiling as he saw an ambulance. *That was quick*, he thought, but then, there had been an enormous explosion. Maybe they'd been a few streets away. Maybe they'd just raced straight here. There were people milling about in the street, most of them looking on, most of them not from the emergency services, but a paramedic ran up to him.

'Are you okay, sir?' the man asked.

'Ann. Check Ann. Quick.' Dermott dropped to the ground.

The paramedic walked over, looked down at her, and then shouted to his colleague. Soon, there was a trolley arriving. Dermott breathed a sigh of relief, but his side was aching. He'd badly bruised himself getting out of that building. He tried to raise himself to his feet.

'I need to go back in and check for others.'

'No, you don't,' said the paramedic, who now had a colleague beside him. The two of them put Ann on the trolley, pushing her towards the back of the ambulance. 'You in here too, sir. I think you've punctured something.'

Dermott was led up into the back of the ambulance. Once they'd secured Ann in place on the stretcher, the doors were closed behind them. Dermott noted both paramedics were there.

'Shouldn't we get going to the hospital?' he said.

'We'll get there in time,' said the man. Dermott collapsed on one seat at the side of the ambulance, but as he looked up, he saw the paramedic standing over Ann. The man had a scalpel in his hand.

'Does she need surgery? We should go then. We should get to the hospital.'

'You'll all need surgery,' said the paramedic standing beside Dermott. Suddenly the man reached down, put a hand under Dermott's chin, and pulled it backwards, exposing his neck. 'And you'll get yours for free on the NHS,' said the paramedic, who slashed a knife across Dermott's throat.

Life passed before Dermott quickly and then went. The last thing he heard were his own gargles. Across from him, the man cut Ann's throat as well.

'Give me a hand with this one,' said the paramedic, standing over Ann. The other one joined him. Together they picked her up, stood her at the back door of the ambulance, propping her there. They then pulled over Dermott and propped him beside her. Quickly, they opened the doors. Two bodies fell out onto the roadside, and the ambulance was closed.

A young police officer had just arrived on the scene. He'd only been in the force two years, but as he stepped out of the car, he watched the ambulance doors open and the two bodies fall onto the ground. They hit with a considerable thump, but there was no life in those who had dropped. The door of the ambulance was closed, and he saw some blood running out of the back of it. Blue lights went on, and it sped off, much to the shock of the officer.

He did well, getting the number plate, writing it down in his book. He shouted into his radio what had happened and the number plate of the ambulance that had disappeared.

The rest of the scene was a mess. As the firemen arrived and through the next twenty-four hours worked at the building to make it secure, the count of bodies went up. Several streets away on a piece of waste ground, an ambulance had exploded, practically blown to smithereens. The city centre was in chaos, and the police tried to lock everywhere down for the first couple of hours. Things, however, went quiet after the first twenty minutes. Everything now was just panic and shock.

Everyone in the building that the bomb was in was dead. On the streets, several people were treated for flying glass. Someone was unfortunate enough to be near the ambulance when it exploded. They would spend several nights in hospital because of the wounds received.

Meanwhile, in London, a tall man, thin too, who looked like an old English gent, sat behind a desk in a secret office. He read the reports of what had happened and gave very little away except that his fist closed ever so slightly in the most understated moment of rage ever not seen.

Chapter 02

Kirsten Stewart was glum. Her boyfriend had disappeared. He'd gone from trying to commit suicide to leaving the institution. He was in denial, apparently going rogue. It had been a cryptic message from Anna Hunt, and she didn't specify exactly what *rogue* meant. She was needing clarity, needing to make sure of what rumours she had heard.

Kirsten was struggling to comprehend life at this moment. She had gone from being an ordinary detective—a constable underneath the tutelage of Seoras Macleod, a man she deeply respected, who had told her she needed to move out from under him—to being an operative for the British Secret Service, before going freelance. He had helped her get into the Service, and she had been good at what she did. But the Service had eroded her—her morals, her standing.

She thought about the number of people that she had dispatched. She thought about how she'd found Craig, and how he'd had his legs basically blown off. About how that had changed him, how bitter he'd become. You didn't get that if you became a baker or a schoolteacher. At least, it was less likely. Much, much less likely.

Kirsten wished that the cup in front of her had been filled with a large triple vodka or something that would just melt her mind and take the pain away. Instead, it was coffee. It was black and wasn't really that good. She was only drinking it because she didn't want to sit around the house moping.

Kirsten had struggled to find Craig. Everywhere she'd looked, every lead she'd tried, nothing. He'd escaped from his institution and gone to ground. The rumours Anna Hunt had provided may have been true, but the very leads that she'd given her, the odd contact or name, had turned out to be overstated. There was nowhere to go with them. Craig was gone.

She slept alone at night. Part of her thought about moving on. Part of her thought maybe she should just find another man. Someone to give her some love, to give her some affection, someone she could have some fun with. But Craig was unfinished business, and she would not give up on him that easily.

If he'd walked away, it would've been easier. If he simply had said, 'I don't want you in my life anymore. We can't be what we were,' it would've hurt, but at least it would've been a clean cut. Instead, he was rogue—and if he was rogue, by Anna's definition, that meant he was a danger to the country.

Yes, if it had been anybody else, someone she wasn't connected with, she could have walked away. But Craig was part of her, and part of her couldn't be allowed to turn rogue. Maybe she could save him. After all, it was the injury that caused this. He hadn't been like this before the injury.

She stared down at the bacon roll. Why did people leave the fat—well, so fatty? Why didn't they crisp it. Crispy bacon? Bacon was meant to crunch when you bit through the roll.

Was that not the point? The bacon was too thick, and this roll sliced as if you were hacking off a chunk of meat, not a sliver of bacon. She pushed it away from her.

Damn Godfrey. Damn him. It had been Godfrey's interference with the Russians that had caused Craig to lose his legs, and that was where Kirsten put the blame for everything. And yet she knew he'd be calling at some point. She needed Godfrey. She knew she needed him if she was ever going to find Craig. Life on your own wasn't easy. It was much harder to discover things, much harder without a network to understand all the players.

Her mobile rang. Kirsten looked at the number. She didn't recognise it. Well, that said something.

'Hello?'

'Kirsten, it's Anna.'

'Have you found something?'

'No,' said Anna. 'Do you read the news or are you still moping?'

'Glasgow,' said Kirsten. 'What happened?'

'We need to meet. I take it you're still in Inverness.'

'Yes,' said Kirsten. 'Where are you?'

'The islands on the River Ness. Half an hour. You close enough?'

'Yes,' said Kirsten. The call was ended. Kirsten left her disappointing bacon roll and coffee and walked across town to the River Ness that gave the city its name. The islands had bridges out to them. Kirsten had been there before, standing, watching the river flow past. The rain had been prevalent, so the river would be running fast.

It took her thirty-five minutes to walk there. It was raining, but she didn't care. Her long black hair sitting on top of her

11

leather jacket, soaked through and forming into large thick strands. When she approached one of the islands, she saw a figure sporting an enormous umbrella. Underneath was a long grey coat, but the shape of the man gave him away. Always thin and wiry. Kirsten walked towards Godfrey, looking around to see where the protection was. She spotted at least three of them there to look after him.

'Good morning, Miss Stewart,' he said.

'You can dispense with the formalities. You obviously need me. What's up?'

'As you will. I have found that formalities make things go along smoother, but if that's what you want.'

'What do you need? Glasgow?'

'Glasgow. Leicester. Portsmouth. Three of our so-called secret offices blown to smithereens. A bomb each time, no survivors. More than that, in Glasgow, we got two out. They went into the back of an ambulance and had their throats slit and were then subsequently dumped on the road. We're talking about people who make sure the job is done. Professionals.'

'Not just random terrorists,' said Kirsten. 'Terrorists would plant the bomb and get out of there. Why hang about to cause further damage?'

'Also, why would you target us unless you knew we were there? The facade we put up with our offices. They're all boring. Well, let's blow up an employment bureau. A launderette. It makes no sense other than we were targeted, which makes me wonder how they knew.'

'Russians?' asked Kirsten.

'No,' said Godfrey. 'Here. Stand under the umbrella.'

'I think I'm wet enough,' she said. 'A little more will not

matter.'

Godfrey studied her for a moment. 'Are you fit and able?'

'Very!' said Kirsten. 'I'm in the shape of my life.'

Godfrey ignored the sarcasm.

'Anna Hunt is investigating Portsmouth and Leicester, but she'd be far stretched to be up in Glasgow as well. Truth is, I need you to investigate this. Obviously, we'll pay you as usual and you'll have the Service at your disposal.'

'Why me?' asked Kirsten.

'I told you. Anna Hunt can't cover off all three.'

'Anna Hunt isn't your only operative,' said Kirsten. 'Something like this, you would keep in-house. Why hire it out?'

'Because you're good,' said Godfrey.

'I know I'm good. I don't need you to tell me I'm good,' said Kirsten. 'I need you to tell me why you're hiring me.'

'Is my money not good enough?' asked Godfrey.

'Your money's fine. I need to understand what's going on.'

'What's going on is, I have had three places bombed and I need to find out who did it. The bomb dynamics have the signature of a Mark Lamb. I don't know if you're aware of him, but I'm sure that the file will be made available to you on request. He's been recently seen in the Perth area.'

'Mark Lamb, Perth area. It's fine. I'll talk to Justin, get the details. I take it he is on this.'

'He is indeed, and you can talk to Justin. But just Justin, Anna, and me. Don't talk to anyone else. I take it we have a deal.'

Godfrey turned and began to walk away.

'Wait,' said Kirsten.

'Wait? I said we have a deal.'

'And I've said nothing yet.' Kirsten stood in the rain and

watched as Godfrey turned back round and walked towards her. She stepped over to the edge of the island and pointed down to the river.

'See that there?' she said. 'Imagine trying to stop that. You could get somebody to build a dam. You could get somebody to divert the water. But if you really want to stop it, you need to know what's going on upstream. That's because the force of the water keeps coming, and if it keeps coming, you got to put the water somewhere. You can't just hold it back or everything rises.'

'I think I understand how rivers work,' said Godfrey.

'You understand how these things work,' said Kirsten. 'First, why am I only talking to certain people? Why have I been put on a short leash in that respect? Second, why do you need me?'

'I am not obliged to tell you any of that.'

'I'm not obliged to make a deal with you either.'

'You're not stupid, Miss Stewart. You understand rightly why I'm telling you not to talk to others.'

'I think you are wondering if this information that allowed them to plant the bombs came from in-house.'

'When the bombs went up, certain people were downstairs. We're still picking up the pieces of them. We're trying to see if everyone who should have been there was there.'

'You think you've got problems on the inside. If you've got problems on the inside, I suggest you pull people in, interrogate, and find out,' said Kirsten. She saw Godfrey glance across at her. 'You've done that, haven't you? You've been pulling people in. Hell, you don't know what's going on.'

'Do we have a deal?'

'Yes,' said Kirsten.

'Good,' said Godfrey. 'And I know you're thinking, "is Craig involved?" That's why you just said yes. Truthfully?'

'You're using a lot of unfamiliar words these days,' said Kirsten.

'Truthfully, I don't know. Truthfully, I don't know a lot. That's why you're here. I told you, you're good.'

'Maybe the best,' said Kirsten. It wasn't a boast. It was a very simple statement.

'I sent the best to Leicester and Portsmouth. Pick up Glasgow for me. Chase down Mark Lamb. Find out who planted that bomb. Find out why they're coming for us. Who told them? Find out as much as you can. Understand?'

'Understood,' said Kirsten.

'Oh, and, Miss Stewart, you're authorised to use all force to stop any further attacks and also to bring any of these people that did it to justice. I've currently lost twenty-five of my people.'

'Well, there'd be twenty-two if someone was in on it.'

'Whether I lose them to a bomber, or I lose them to another side, I have lost them and I'm not taking that lightly.'

Kirsten watched as Godfrey walked off the island and took the bridge over to the road at the far side. A car had pulled up for him and he flapped his umbrella, shaking off the water before stepping inside. Meanwhile, Kirsten stood in the rain and tilted her head back, closing her eyes, but allowing the water to fall onto her face.

The sad thing she noted was, as Godfrey asked about these things, she'd become alive. The Service, everything with it was exciting. She'd been to many places. Yes, she'd almost died a few times, but she'd lived. It was exciting.

Part of her thought about going back to that quiet life with Craig. The two of them had planned it and for a while, it had

15

been fun. Kirsten wondered what fun it would be in the long run. Anna Hunt was still in the business. Why? She was on her own.

It was a drug. She was addicted to it. She knew what she'd say to Godfrey from the moment he asked and she told herself it was about Craig. In truth, it wasn't. This entire way of life dragged her in. As much as she said she would like to leave it, as much as she talked about how it wasn't an authentic way to live, there was part of Kirsten that loved it.

She turned, soaking, and walked off the island to make her way back to her apartment. There was a sudden spring in Kirsten's step. She was on a mission. She was alive again.

Chapter 03

Kirsten returned to her flat, soaked to the skin but becoming more alive by the second. After a quick shower, she changed and called Justin Chivers on the phone.

'How are things?' asked Chivers.

'You know it's not a social call. I'm sure you've been briefed.'

'So, you're looking into Mark Lamb.'

'I am, indeed. I believe that you've got some information.'

'Look, I'll send you through the usual stuff and also a connection to Mark Lamb. It's tenuous, but it's the best I've got at the moment. He seems to have gone to ground. To be honest, it seems to be more than he normally would've done.'

'What do you mean?' asked Kirsten.

'This guy, he's a bomber. Yes, he can hide out, but we could find him if we really wanted to and pulled out all the stops. Well, we've done that and all I've got is a tenuous link. I think somebody else is hiding him or helping him to hide.'

'Okay,' said Kirsten. 'If that's where we start, that's where we start. Send it through. I'll be in touch when I've got something.'

'Before you go,' said Justin suddenly.

'What?' asked Kirsten. Justin's voice sounded tentative.

'Have you seen anything?'

'What do you mean by "seen anything?"'

'Have you noticed anything unusual?'

'I'm not sure I follow you. Could you expand?'

'Hang on,' he said. 'I'll send you that stuff through, but I need to call you from elsewhere. Not comfortable explaining it here.'

Kirsten could understand this. She had called up on what would've been a confidential line, a line that would've been protected, and yet Justin wasn't happy. But Justin knew his business, and Kirsten would not argue with him about what was happening. Especially since she didn't yet know.

She sat in front of her laptop, waiting for the email to arrive. As she did so, she thought about the last conversation she'd had with Godfrey. He had been anxious. Now Justin was nervous. Anna Hunt was her usual business sense-like self, but maybe that was just Anna. Since nothing had come through, she stood up and turned to make herself a coffee. As soon as she put the kettle on to boil, she felt her mobile phone ringing.

'Hello?' The number in front of her was not recognised.

'It's Justin. I needed to call you on a prepay. Make sure nobody traces this.'

'Why?' asked Kirsten.

'Have you seen anything unusual within the Service?'

'Well, all things are often pretty unusual in the Service.'

'No, I mean unusual. Really out of the ordinary. Have you seen anything?'

'I just met with Godfrey a while ago, and he's about the most unusual I've ever seen. He seemed tentative, unassured. It's not like him, but then again, he has had three stations blown up. I can understand why he'd be anxious.'

'You said tentative. Godfrey has been anxious before,' said Justin, 'but never tentative. He always just acts; he always looks self-assured even if he's worried.'

'And?'

'He's brought many people in for conversations.'

'Godfrey talks to people all the time. What's the big deal with conversations?'

'From those who I have seen, or got something coherent back from, the conversations have been almost like an interrogation, just with no physical force being put on them.'

'Well, you've just had three bombs go through three bases. I mean, what do you expect from the man?'

'That's the thing. It was starting before that, as if he expected something would be amiss.'

'Something's definitely amiss if you get three stations taken out at once.'

'There's more than that,' said Justin. His voice was going quieter now, and Kirsten was unsure of where exactly he was. 'Things at the top level, I don't know the best way to put this, they're more confidential. More things are wrapped up tight than should be.'

'You're right, you don't know how to put this. I don't know what you're talking about.'

'It's like this,' said Justin. 'Normally, you see bits of paper going here and there, information. There's a certain classification on it. Now those levels are usually too high for some of the stuff that's irrelevant.'

'What do you make of that?' asked Kirsten, unsure what to think about it herself.

'I think he's testing; he's trying out the waters. That's why he's bringing people in. That's why he's talking to them. He's trying to see who's leaking things from the inside. There's no way they could have put bombs in those places without somebody leaking it.'

'What can you do about it?' asked Kirsten. 'Or do you indeed need to do anything about it?'

'Godfrey runs a tight ship,' said Justin. 'I've always known him to. I've always seen him being in charge. All parts of the beast on the move, and all looked after by him. He's the master, the one at the top. He's the one that knows what everybody's doing. But I'm getting the feeling he's unsure. There's something rotten within the organisation and he's struggling to root it out. I think that's why he's had all these interviews. He even brought me in. I think that's why he's reached out to you.'

'Me?' said Kirsten. 'What, because I'm his best buddy?'

'No, because you're outside. He can trust you, or at least he believes he can.'

'What's that meant to mean?'

'Well,' said Justin, 'you're quite straight, aren't you? You say what you're going to do, and you do it. At the moment, he's being undercut. He also knows you're good, when combined with me, obviously.'

'You've voiced all this anxiety to me,' said Kirsten. 'You're telling me all these problems. What exactly do you want me to do with it?'

'I want to meet. I want to meet because—well, there are things I'm not even going to say on a phone.'

'Okay, we'll meet. Tell me where and when.'

'I'll need to work on that. I've got too much on to be seen disappearing. What I will do, I'll get in touch with you as soon as I can. What I would say is watch your back.'

'I thought that's what we always did.'

'I mean, watch your back from everyone; trust no one,' said Justin. 'Godfrey is looking to clean house because he's worried and he doesn't know who the culprits are. There's no way any of us should be trusting anyone for now.'

'You're trusting me, aren't you?'

'That's the dilemma, isn't it?' said Justin. 'At some point, you have to trust somebody.'

'Don't worry, I always do,' said Kirsten. 'Tell me when you're ready to meet me.'

'Will do.'

'In the meantime, I'll check over that stuff you're giving me.'

Kirsten printed off an email that came through from Justin and sat on her sofa, legs outstretched on the small coffee table in front of her. The detail was some four pages, giving a background history of Mark Lamb. He'd been a bomber of some repute. Heavily involved out in Spain, where he'd grown up, before being linked with various terrorist organisations around the world. He made a name for himself as the Perfectionist, someone who could always deliver the right size of bomb, the right way to set it off, and the right way to make it untraceable.

Of course, certain ones were traced as potential handiwork, but never proved to be he. Certainly, it was never he who planted it. But he'd been quiet for a while and sources believed that he'd made enough money to start enjoying it. He was a terrorist, but he was not a fanatic. He was in it for the money. In some ways, he was a mercenary. It's just that he knew who to work with. Governments wouldn't have paid him what the terrorists paid him.

Mark Lamb had so many potential buyers. Life was simple.

He turned down jobs as much as took them. The annex was a list of sightings. Kirsten ran down the page, reading carefully who had made the observation, and where Mark Lamb had been in Scotland. He'd also been in Portsmouth and near Leicester. He'd been seen on the west side of Scotland, but no one was sure exactly what for. There were no bases on the west side of Scotland due to how sparse it was. The authorities determined that there wasn't enough action to warrant a base.

Kirsten had to concur. She covered most of the west coast from Inverness when she worked for the Service. With the Glasgow base running now as well and having incorporated the Inverness base, there was more than enough cover. Mark Lamb had various associates initially labelled with him. Kirsten noticed that all of them were dead, dispatched after the bomb had gone off in the area. The Scottish contacts were all dead except for one person, Danny Kyle.

The problem was, nobody seemed to know who Danny Kyle was. Ostensibly, he was a motor trader, and he had a yard, but no one had seen him at the yard for several months. Just what did he do? Where was his money coming from? Currently, he was based in a Perth hotel, and Kirsten noted he had spoken of the Perfectionist, and that was why he was being brought into the equation.

Kirsten would need to set off for Perth, and she went into her room to pack her bag. She wanted to travel light, and so took out a small rucksack, packing it with clothes, and was ready to go in half an hour. She brought a couple of handguns with her, and enough ammunition, so she believed, and stored it inside the car. Kirsten then made her way across town to an old mixed martial arts ring, a place she'd been brought up in, and where she'd first fought. The drive would be long, and she wanted to loosen up beforehand. Walking through the door, she got a smile from the gym's master.

'Stewie, good to see you.'

Nowhere else was she called Stewie. They didn't do it at work, but here amongst the MMA fighters, she was known as Stewie, the little pocket rocket. She hadn't fought in any competitions in a long while. She was a lot stronger, physically and mentally. Kirsten would only bring attention by winning tournaments. Instead, she came down here to train. She popped into the ladies' changing, came back out in her shorts and top, and began to hit the bags with her feet and her hands for thirty minutes. She went at it almost hell for leather. When she stepped back afterwards, she saw the master looking over at her.

'You beat that thing to a pulp,' he said. 'I take it Craig's not made an appearance yet.' She shook her head. 'Now, that's a pity, but next time, if you'd kindly leave my bag intact.' Kirsten looked at the side of the rather large punch bag. Where she'd connected with her feet, the bag had split.

'Sorry,' she said. 'I'm just—'

'You're over-psyched and over-pumped. Something good happening?' he asked. 'You have a spring in that step. Last couple of weeks I've seen you, you've been very lazy on the footwork, or maybe just slow. Maybe just weighed down with things.'

The man never missed a trick, but Kirsten didn't give him an answer, simply a nod and left. She took a shower in the changing room first and then stepped outside, ready for her drive south. While she went to leave the building, she heard a voice calling for her. 'Stewie, come here a minute.'

She turned back, walking up to her master. 'Look,' he said,

'I don't want to get in your way or that. Can you take advice from an old guy?' he said.

'Of course,' she said.

'Things don't always work out the way we plan, and we can't always put them back together. I see you today. You're pumped, you're hyped, you're thinking you can get somewhere. Understand, somebody always doesn't get somewhere. It's always the case.'

'No, they don't,' said Kirsten.

'Yes, they do. Somebody has to lose. It's the way of the world. I don't know what you're going into now, Stewie. I know you don't talk to me about what you do outside of here, and that's okay. That's your prerogative. You accept words from me regarding what you do in here. Trust me, like in here, when you fight in that ring, there's a winner and there's a loser. When you go into that world, there's always a winner. Maybe one or two, maybe three or four, but for everyone that there is, there'll be a loser on the other side. At least one, usually a lot more. Take care of yourself, Stewie, and if you need anything, you always know where you can come.'

'If I'm needing you with what I'm doing, I think I'm in trouble.' She laughed, but the thought was a good one. She reached up and tapped him on the shoulder. He gave her a shake of the head, opened his arms up wide, and stepped forward.

'You need one of these,' he said. 'I've been watching.' She stepped in close and hugged him. He was right, and she stopped in the hug for longer than she thought she would before stepping back.

'Take care, Stewie. It's important you come back to us.'

'Always,' she said and walked out of the gym straight to her car.

Chapter 04

The drive down to Perth was an uneventful one, with rain being the primary order of the day. The A9 was its usual self; when it was a single lane, it was slow, averaging around fifty miles per hour. Then, when it broke into a dual carriageway, everyone desperately raced to get past.

Kirsten enjoyed the scenery. At first, the open expanse climbing up from Inverness. Then Slochd summit with rocks on either side before heading into what was truly mountain country. They rose high on either side, mainly in browns now, the summer glories disappearing. Once clear of them, the land settled into valleys that wound with rivers, trees flanking either side. By the time she'd got to Burnham, she was ready to stop her drive.

Perth was busy. Kirsten wasn't sure why. There seemed to be a fair number of tourists about. Maybe the popularity of the Highlands was getting stronger every year. She found the hotel that Danny Kyle was rumoured to be staying in and waited in the lobby, drinking three cups of coffee over two hours. But the coffee drinking wasn't in vain.

She saw Danny Kyle coming into the lobby and heading out of the door. The picture in the notes from Justin Chivers was excellent, and Kyle was easy to spot. Kirsten tailed him until he got into a car. She walked past it and dropped a tracker onto the car.

She turned the corner, pulled out her phone, and made sure the tracker was activated before strolling back to her own car. She trailed Danny for quite a distance, a good half mile behind him. The map inside her car showed her he was heading to a country house near to the outskirts of Perth. From half a mile behind and seeing that the car had stopped at the country house, Kirsten took up a position watching with a long-range scope. She had thought about getting a drone to get up close. The trouble was they were so blooming noisy, certainly by surveillance standards. So, instead, she watched through the eyeglass.

The country house wasn't particularly impressive, being a rather small affair. Danny was waiting outside it, leaning against the boot of the car. This was despite the light drizzle that was in the air. Kirsten thought it rather strange that he didn't go up and knock. Another larger car arrived. A chauffeur went to the rear of the car, pulled out a wheelchair, and positioned it beside the rear passenger door. It opened, and the chair was pulled closer by the occupant. He slid himself in. Kirsten recognised the shape of the man straight away. Her heart beat fast.

The man turned and wheeled himself forward to shake hands with Danny Kyle. Another man in an expensive suit followed him before they made their way over to the front door of the house. It had steps leading up to it. Craig, in his wheelchair, could not get up them. Instead, a butler opened the door, then indicated that they should come round to the side of the house.

There was a conservatory. Doors were opened, and Craig

wheeled himself in. Kirsten was quite glad because the conservatory had large glass windows allowing her to see in, whereas the rest of the house was impenetrable, and she would have had to come up closer for a better look.

It was a long discussion with Craig and the wealthy man talking a lot to Danny Kyle. Kyle spoke little, but he took a lot of notes. Craig looked vehement, reacting to several things that were said.

Kirsten focused in closely and with her scope, could get a clear view of Craig's face. Inside she was melting, struggling. This was the man she'd fallen for, the man she thought she was going to live her life with, but here he was conspiring with bad people. She didn't know who or why, but she knew. She was tasked with investigating, and she remembered Godfrey's words that all force was permitted. Godfrey wouldn't say that unless he expected there to be a requirement.

Kirsten was lying in the grass, scope pointed towards the conservatory. When she heard a noise, it was a low whir and worryingly close. Kirsten feared she knew what it was.

She took her head away from the eyepiece and turned, looking up to see a drone passing above her. It went one way and then came back the other. She returned to her eyepiece, zooming in as best she could and seeing if she could pick up any words. The three men were no amateurs. Often, they covered their faces. Sometimes their backs were to the windows so they couldn't be seen. All Kirsten had at the moment were three people meeting in a country house. Craig, another who was wealthy, and Danny Kyle, who was linked to the bomber Mark Lamb.

Kirsten kept watching as the debate raged inside the conservatory. She had seen these sorts of discussions before.

Clearly, there was some planning, something going on, but why Danny Kyle; why Craig? Who was the other guy? She attached her phone to the scope, zooming in on each and taking photographs.

What was Craig doing there? Why was he getting involved in this? She thought he was angry about the legs. She thought he was angry about Godfrey, but that didn't make you someone who would blow places up. Innocent colleagues did not do that.

She wanted to say no, but in truth, she didn't know him anymore. The man who was in the institution, the man who broke out, the man who would constantly swear at her, tell her to get out, was not the man she'd fallen for. It had all gone wrong on that holiday. Their idyllic life had changed, and she had never fully recovered from it.

The job took her away from that. At least, it had done going up to Canada, then down to Argentina. But here it was, bringing her back face to face with the issue. Here she would have to confront what Craig would become.

The whirring sound happened again. She flicked her head around to see the drone passing by, but this time, it stopped for too long. Kirsten put her eye back on the scope and watched. They were still having their conversation in the conservatory.

Craig, several times, could be seen trying to get out of his chair as if he was going to stand and make a point and then realising he couldn't. Danny Kyle kept backing down. The rich man just seemed to be, well, there for some unknown reason. He articulated nothing during the most heated times.

Kirsten's scope was suddenly filled when a woman entered the conservatory. She had long blonde hair and a dress that made you think she was out for a night on the town. Oh, she

29

wore it well, and she looked every bit the ounce of a bombshell in it, but she walked with purpose. She walked like someone who was in charge, or at least had a lot of responsibility. Inside of thirty seconds, she spoke to the men in the room, and they cleared out.

The doors opened, Craig wheeling himself out, and Kirsten knew it was time to go. But she didn't. She lingered on him, her scope tracing him as he got back to the car. Only once he was inside did she close the scope up, put it back in her pack, and looked to leave the area.

She was sure they'd left because of her. After all, the drone had stopped. She wasn't worried about it, and the position she was sitting in made any long-distance sniping hard. That's if they even had one trained to shoot that far. Kirsten kept low, her eyes scanning the surrounding countryside. Her car was a little way off, parked close to a set of trees. She'd taken it just off the road, made sure it was hidden from anyone passing by, but it wouldn't take long to discover it if a proper search was done.

She needed to get on the move, but she didn't want to take the line directly from the road. *That's where they will come from. That's where they will look for me, surely. How many will come? How will they track me down?*

There was that whirring sound again. Kirsten looked up and saw the drone moving towards her. She reached inside her jacket, pulled out a handgun with a silencer on it and, with one shot, took down the drone. *Somebody was going to be about three hundred quid out,* she thought, *but better that than me dead.*

She was on the side of a hill, and down below was a wood. If she went to the left-hand side of the hill, she was in open country. There was only one choice. Well, strictly there were two. She could sprint back up over the hill up to where the road was, but if they were already here, she was as good as dead. She turned and made her way down into the trees.

On reaching the small wood at the bottom, she saw it had a river running through the middle of it. *They may bring dogs*, she thought. She could leap into the river, but if she did, she would be noisy while moving along it. On the other hand, it had rocks along either side. You could hide easily.

Hiding in between trees was difficult, especially because of the low branches. Then, running away, you got hit in the face with many branches unless you really crouched down. And if you really crouched down, you couldn't run at pace. No, the play was the river.

Kirsten climbed into the river, ignoring how her boots and leggings were filling with water. She made her way to the other side and clambered up onto some rocks to wait there, listening. There was no drizzle at this time, but there was a stiff wind blowing along. She heard the trees rustle. This was a double-edged sword. They wouldn't hear her. But she could have problems hearing them, too.

Kirsten found a rock formation where, unless they were looking straight at her, she would be obscured. It was like a hidy-hole with only one way in. Trouble with that was there was only one way out. She'd have to see them before they saw her.

Kirsten took an extendable mirror, lifting it up above the rock and scanning, seeing if anyone was walking through the forest. She caught the side of a boot. Then she thought she heard a noise behind her. She spun and looked over. Someone was crawling along the river.

On the other side of the bank, Kirsten looked down. Just in

front of her was a deep pool. Maybe she could go into it. She focused her eyes on the man on the opposite bank. If he kept going like that—.

Quickly, she reached inside her jacket, found the waterproof pocket she had, and placed her gun inside it. She closed it over, zipped her jacket up, and slowly lowered herself into the pond. She pushed down off a rock, feeling the cold water go over her neck and her head. Kirsten slowly counted.

She could hold her breath well, but she needed to do more than hold it well. There were a bunch of reeds ahead of her. She reached out, snapped one, and pulled it down into the water. She broke the other end of it, leaving a long tube. Slowly, she broke the surface with it and then blew out the water, allowing her to have a channel through which to breathe.

Fifteen minutes in that water left her cold, but only then did Kirsten surface. Slowly, she looked around her, and she climbed up over the rocks and onto the bank on that side. She suddenly saw movement on the other bank and stepped behind a tree, peering out from behind it. There were three men discussing. Carefully, she walked away, out through the forest and up towards the road.

It took Kirsten another ten minutes to make her way via the far side of the road up to where her car was parked behind some trees. When she got there, she sat for five minutes, looking to see if anyone would be coming. When no one did, she raced for the car, started it up and drove off. She went the opposite direction from which she'd come in.

Danny Kyle's car still had a tracker on it. She'd find him again. Craig and the wealthy man were gone. She'd had no chance to follow them. Instead, she drove down into Perth to find a basic hotel.

The desk staff looked at her rather strangely, as she slowly marched into the reception, sodden, but they were quick about the room. Once in there, Kirsten retrieved her gun and she had a quick shower.

She checked Danny Kyle's tracker. He was back at the hotel. She would see what he was doing this evening. He'd had a meeting. There'd been words said, strong words. There would be actions following it, but with whom? Would it be said, or sent via emails? Unlikely. Sent by text over phones or would there be a meeting? More likely. Kirsten sat in her room and made herself a coffee, which she sipped. Her brain had been about business, but all the time she felt the punch of her heart. *That was Craig* something said. *Craig was with them. Craig was doing something illegal. Craig was doing something that had killed people. Craig was rogue, rogue.*

What would she do if he truly was rogue? It suddenly occurred to her that she might be facing him. There might come a point when she would have to take him down.

Kirsten didn't cry easily, but she let the tears flow for five minutes. *Let the tears come so that you won't be compromised later. You have to get rid of the emotion. The emotion gets you killed . . . and there was plenty of emotion on this job.*

Chapter 05

Having recovered from her dip in the river, Kirsten made for Danny Kyle's hotel. The tracker on the car showed he was still there. Kirsten waited in the lobby. She was dressed in culottes with a loose top and a scarf around her head, trying to change her appearance from earlier on in the day. No one seemed to give her any notice.

She started reading the papers with a cup of coffee in front of her. That was the good thing about classy hotels. They had somewhere for you to sit, somewhere you could wait. If the target was stopping at one of the cheaper hotels or even the American motel-type places, it was much harder to be inconspicuous. Nobody hung around those places to read the papers, but these classier ones, you got all sorts.

She kept her a watch for anyone else, possibly looking for her. After all, they knew that somebody had been followed, aware that someone was taking an interest in their meeting. The fact that Kirsten didn't even know what their meeting was about was irrelevant. They didn't know that. They would be spooked. Maybe Danny would be spooked, too.

He came out of the hotel lift at around eight o'clock that evening, walked across the lobby, and was immediately met by an elegant brunette. She didn't look ridiculously overdressed. She was no femme fatal, but there was a figure in there. Kirsten reckoned it was the sort of woman a man would likely enjoy. Maybe this was Danny talking to a potential partner, or maybe just a quick one-night stand. The conversation certainly didn't look heavy. After they'd sat down and had a drink in the lobby, Danny escorted the woman into the restaurant.

Kirsten followed and got a table some distance away. The food was rather good. Kirsten ordered dinner, keeping up the pretence of being a fellow diner, and sat for the next two hours watching Danny enjoy himself with the woman. Kirsten always struggled with the idea of the perfect-looking woman. She got annoyed with the concept as she was 'a little spitfire', as they said, compact, not that tall, but full of fight. Yes, she knew she had some curves, but what was it with these taller, thinner, elegant women?

Elegant, my arse! she thought. *Why do they get called elegant? How am I not elegant?* Kirsten knew why. It was probably because she'd rather stand in a pair of track bottoms and a t-shirt than in any classy dress.

Kirsten ordered coffee after she'd finished her meal, and sat almost chewing on it. Danny and the woman seemed to get along fine. There were plenty of laughs. Kirsten thought it was false, though, especially from the woman.

Kirsten stood up and walked past the couple in the pretence that she was going to the ladies' toilets. As she passed by, she caught a picture on her phone of the woman. When she got to the ladies' toilets, she sat down and sent the picture off to Justin Chivers. Kirsten didn't hang about, but returned to her own table to chew on her coffee again.

Most people thought working for the Service would be

glamorous. It would be all action. Yes, there was a fair bit of action. Yet Kirsten remembered all the times during surveillance—sitting, waiting, watching other people enjoy themselves while she had to sit there pretending to be enjoying herself. Pretending to have a good time at whatever it was she was doing. Instead, she was focused on trying to work out people's intentions, trying to catch the odd word as she lip read.

There was nothing in this conversation, nothing about anything. One word she caught Danny speak was referring to the woman's body. Danny was telling her a joke. She was laughing, insisting that he was one of the funniest men alive. She wondered if he was paying her because she really didn't see the evidence for this thought.

The couple eventually stood up after they had drunk the best part of two bottles of wine. Danny seemed to move rather haphazardly, but the woman was solid. She was walking perfectly straight. Kirsten looked at what they'd drunk.

How much had she had and how much had he put down? Kirsten remembered him filling his glass several times. Yes, he'd filled hers, but never from a standing start. Never was that glass empty. Maybe she was just being a pro about her business. If she was a lady of the night, an escort, it would be her duty to perform later on. Maybe this was how she ensured that. Stay sober. Or maybe being sober kept her safe. She could flee if anything got out of hand.

Kirsten didn't know. She'd never been involved in that type of business. She watched the couple walk from the restaurant to the lobby, making their way to the lift. That was Danny Kyle for the night, up to bed with some woman. Could Kirsten go back to her own hotel? She could set an alarm on the tracker, and if the car moved, then she could come back. It didn't stop him disappearing off for food the next morning or getting picked up by someone. What time would he be up? This was covered, so maybe she'd go back and sleep.

She felt the vibration from her phone. Taking it out, Kirsten looked at a message from Justin Chivers. The woman with Danny Kyle was an assassin, usually highly paid and someone who could kill without upsetting the apple cart. He'd be found in his room the next morning.

Kirsten quickly stood up from the table, walked over, and paid her bill quickly. Then she went over to the front desk.

'Excuse me,' she said. 'I think there was a gentleman with a woman. I think his name was Kyle, Danny Kyle. It's just I think he's left something on the table. I could drop it into him on my way up.'

'We could do that, Madam,' said the rather helpful concierge.

'No, no, no. It's no trouble at all. Just tell me the room and the floor. I'll drop it in.'

'329,' said the man, 'The highest floor.'

Kirsten thanked him and headed for the lift. Fortunately, the man at the desk hadn't realised she wasn't staying there, or maybe he just assumed she was another woman about her business. She wondered how many escorts had arrived at a hotel. A whole other life that she never realised existed or rather didn't realise to what extent it existed. She wasn't sure she really wanted to know.

Catching the lift, Kirsten let it stop at the third floor and stepped out. Slowly, she made her way along the corridor to room 329. She rapped on the door gently.

'Who is it?' asked a woman's voice.

'Apologies for disturbing you,' said Kirsten, 'But one of you,

I think, the gentleman left something at the table downstairs. I'm bringing it up for him.'

'Oh, that's very kind of you. What is it?' asked the woman.

Damn it, thought Kirsten. *She'll know I'm not genuine.* She reached inside of her top and withdrew her weapon. There was a silencer on the end, but her mind was racing with ideas of how to achieve what she wanted to do quietly.

What she wanted was to get Danny Kyle out of there, into a safe house, and interrogate him. After all, whoever he was working with had decided to despatch him or somebody else had. Kirsten did not know what was going on yet, so taking Kyle in would be the best of both worlds. However, if she didn't get him in alive, she'd be stuck.

'It's a cufflink,' said Kirsten suddenly. *Would the woman check? What would she do? What was going on inside? Had she already killed Danny Kyle? Was she in the throes of it? Had she not even started? Would she come looking for the cufflink to bring it back in? Would she try to haul Kirsten in? Despatch her in the room? Would Kirsten get away with standing in front of the door, even? She could look through the peephole, see her there, and shoot her through the door.*

All these thoughts raced into Kirsten's mind, and inside of a couple of seconds, her decision was made. She fired a quick shot into the handle door, then kicked it, sending it open. Inside, she saw the woman with an arm around Danny Kyle's neck throttling him, while grabbing a weapon from inside her bag. Kirsten hit her with two shots, straight to the forehead, and she dropped to the floor, causing a thud when she hit the carpet.

Kirsten shut the door behind her, running forward towards Danny Kyle, who had been choking. He was utterly naked on his knees beside the bed. Kirsten could see the shock on his face. Clearly, he was expecting a night of something entirely different, but he was in for a bigger shock.

'Are you okay?' asked Kirsten.

'Who are you?' he blurted, desperately spitting the words out.

'It doesn't matter now.'

Kirsten looked down at the bag the woman had taken the gun out of. Inside, she saw a small device with a button. A panic button. Somebody was coming.

'We need to move,' said Kirsten.

'I'm stark bollock naked,' said the man.

'And you'll be a dead bollock naked man in a minute. You need to move.'

'I'm not going anywhere until I get my pants on,' he said. Kirsten put her gun on the side of his neck.

'Move.' He stood up, and she put a hand onto the back of his neck, holding it tight.

'Ah, that hurts.'

'Then damn well move when I tell you to.'

There was no other way out of the hotel room. She needed to be out of that door quickly and moving off the floor. Kirsten raced towards the door, pulled it back with her gun hand, and quickly peered out. There was no one in the corridor.

She dragged Danny through with her and headed down to the far end of the corridor, where she saw an emergency exit sign. As they ran past one of the later rooms, a door suddenly opened. A woman walked out and shrieked loudly as Kirsten tore past with Danny. She heard the words, 'Oh, dear God,' from a man, but instead of stopping to apologise, she sped up. Arriving at the end of the corridor, Kirsten kicked open the door to the emergency stairs. She instantly stepped back out, throwing Danny across the hall.

Two shots rang out, smashing the glass of the door, but Kirsten was down low to avoid them. She pushed open the door again and more shots rang out, but she crawled forward on her belly. Kirsten then fired several shots, still with the silencer on, at whoever was down below. She heard the shots ricochet off the wall.

They would duck, she thought. Kirsten stood up. There was no one there. She tried to peer further down the stairs. Again, there was no one there. She waited. Someone moved, went to stand up. Kirsten shot twice in quick succession. A man tumbled on the stairs. She called back at the open door and shouted Danny through from the corridor. There was a ruckus in the corridor, a woman still screaming, a man complaining loudly, but Danny stepped through.

She grabbed him by the neck again. 'With me, down the stairs, down the stairs.' They dashed down the hard steps. Kirsten wondered how many people would converge on the hotel. When she'd been spotted by the drone, there were three. If there were three, they'd have to cover exits. Having shot this one, the current route may be their best way out.

Ideally, she'd have liked to have gone down, peering around each corner, checking here and there, making sure that the route was safe. She didn't want to let go of Danny, and she didn't want to wait. If she did, she could be pinned from behind and from in front. Then there'd be no escape. It wasn't as if she could hide behind Danny. She needed him alive.

They tore down the stairs, round the next corner and round the next one. When she took the one after that, a man came into view. He fired. She thrust Danny forward, and he tumbled down the solid steps. Kirsten leaned back, heard the shot go past, and then stepped forward with two hands on her weapon and fired. The first one caught the man in the shoulder. The second one caught him somewhere else on the chest. He fell down. Kirsten rushed forward, hurdling Danny, before putting two bullets in the head of the man who attacked her.

'Get up. Get your arse out of this door,' she hissed.

Kirsten grabbed Danny by the neck again when he stood up, and they tore off out of the emergency exit into the car park. There was a commotion outside, people screaming as Kirsten hauled Danny towards her car. She unlocked it, told him to get in and jumped in the driver's side.

She started the car and drove off, almost amused by the way Danny was putting on his seatbelt. A car went to block her, but Kirsten swerved around it and then was out on the main road. She didn't hold back, driving as fast as she could, hurtling round every bend. Taking a random choice of lefts and rights, Kirsten kept going until she was out of sight in the Inverness countryside.

'Where are we going?' asked Danny. 'Who the hell are you?'

'Well, there's a lot we don't know about each other,' said Kirsten. 'But I'm going to take you somewhere where at the very least I'm going to put a blanket on you, and we're going to have a chat.' Kirsten had transferred the gun to her left hand, and it was now pointing at Danny. 'You just sit there until we get there,' she said, 'or I'll have to silence you.'

'Are you a friend?'

'I really don't know,' said Kirsten. 'I really don't know.'

41

Chapter 06

Kirsten drove down the small track with only her sidelights on, not wanting to use the full headlights. She was pretty sure she'd shaken off her pursuers, but she still had a gun pointed at Danny Kyle beside her. The man was sitting with his hands between his legs, stark naked and beginning to shiver.

'Where are we going?'

'Shut up,' said Kirsten calmly. 'You'll find out when we get there. If you're lucky, I might have a rug. Well, I can't say the fleas haven't been on it.'

Danny Kyle was shivering, and Kirsten wasn't sure if it was the cold of the night or the terror that came with being pursued. He'd obviously thought he was in for the night of his life, but when the woman had turned, Danny had got the fright of his life instead. He had Kirsten to thank for rescuing him. Yet, he was probably sitting wondering, was she a friend or a foe? Well, she certainly wasn't a friend, but she might be somebody who needed to keep him alive.

The track she turned down swung hard left, and she remembered to be cautious about this bit. There was a drop of some thirty feet on the left-hand side and the path was extremely narrow for a car. She navigated it slowly and then round another bend was the shack. From the outside, it looked completely run down. Which was as it should be.

It had taken her a while to get the aesthetic right. It had also taken her months to find the right place. The building had been some sort of fallout shelter built by an absolute nutter. When she first found it, it was concreted on the top and it was quite clear it was a new build, something with purpose. She had erected wood around it to make it look like an old shack, had given it a window and broken most of the glass. The charity shop visit had supplied those rather bleak net curtains.

She drove the car around to the rear of the shack so anyone approaching wouldn't be able to see it. Not that anyone approached out here. In the summer months, when the wind died down, the midges were everywhere. It was the last place she wanted to be and in winter, the trek to it was more than enough to put off any wayward explorer.

'Out,' she said.

'Out? Where?' spat Danny.

'There's a gun on the side of your neck. I said out.' He stepped out, still clutching himself between his legs and bow-legged, walked forward towards the shack.

'Open the door,' she said. He did so. Inside was a wooden panelled wall section with a door in it.

Kirsten felt around on the ground and then produced a large brass key. She turned it in the door's lock, opened the door, and sent Danny through. On the other side, on the floor, was a brass handle, a ring-pull that lifted a trapdoor in the floor. Kirsten sent him in the revealed void. Once she had followed him down, Kirsten illuminated some battery-operated lights.

'Where's this?' he asked.

'This is where you and me are going to have a chat. Sit down there.'

She pointed to a wooden chair, and Danny reluctantly sat down. She took some rope, tied him to the chair before taking a blanket and wrapping it around him. There was a small gas cooker with a vent pipe above it. Kirsten looked around at some tins on the side of a shelf. *Soup*, she thought. *She could do with some soup. Maybe Danny could too. Might help get him talking.*

He watched her closely as she warmed up the soup and poured it into two cups. She drank hers first, letting his cool. The warmth was good. As much as Kirsten was used to violence, there was always a period afterward when your heart had to slow down. The beating eased, and the toll of the moment took its course. Often, she would look for some comfort then. It used to be Craig. When he wasn't around, something hot, coffee, a meal of some sort. Something to do so you didn't shake.

She brought the soup over to Danny.

'I don't want your bloody soup.'

'I'm not sure when you're going to be eating, so maybe you should have some of it.' He reluctantly agreed, and she poured some of it into him.

'Quite a night,' she said. 'That woman, did you book her through an agency?'

He scowled at her.

'I'm not sure you picked the right agency. She was an assassin.'

'I got the gist of that. The bit where she tried to kill me.'

'I think she tried to kill you because it had gone wrong—your meeting earlier on in the day.'

She glanced at Danny's face. He was trying to conceal everything but the eyes flickered; the lips pursed ever so slightly.

'Yes,' she said, 'That one, that meeting. The one with the man in the wheelchair and the posh guy. I saw it and they saw me, so I'm probably the reason they intercepted your hooker and put an assassin in her place. Oh, don't worry about your hooker. I mean, they probably just paid her off. It's a bit much to kill a working girl like that when she's done nothing. Attracts too much attention anyway. These people aren't nice people, are they?'

Danny looked at her, a little bemused.

'You're wondering who I am,' said Kirsten. 'Well, I'm going to tell you, but you're going to tell me who the wheelchair man and the other guy were. Why were you meeting them?'

He shook his head.

'Quiet, eh?' said Kirsten. 'Can I explain how this is going to happen? I'm going to ask you questions here and I'm going to interrogate you. To be honest, I will not beat you up. I will not hit you because if you don't talk to me and give me the information, you'll be going somewhere else where they will torture you. They know how to extract information and they'll do it and maybe not in a very subtle way.

'I can't guarantee your survival, but that's okay because I don't work for them. I just get paid by them. They haven't asked me to interrogate you. I'm looking for somebody else. You just happen to be in the way, and I need to know about the wheelchair man and the posh man. So, talk to me or talk to them. I bring you soup. I guarantee they'll bring you pain. Either that or they'll drug you so badly, you'll lose your mind. I'm not having my heartstrings pulled here,' said Kirsten. 'I don't particularly like you, so no shakes from me.'

She watched his face intently. He swore under his breath. 'I don't know the wheelchair man. Honestly, I don't. He came along; he works for those people.'

'What people?'

'The people I've been involved with. I'm running as an intermediary for Mark Lamb. He's doing some work for them. I pass messages and find out what they want.'

'What is it they want?'

'Bombs. I'm not sure one hundred percent what for, but they want bombs. They've had a consignment already. They've used them. I know because I saw it in the news. Glasgow. Couple down in England. Mark knows how to build bombs.'

'He truly does,' said Kirsten. 'Why are you talking to the wheelchair man?'

'Because of the other guy. He's part and parcel of them. He brought the wheelchair man to me. We were talking specifications.'

'What are the specifications?'

'Bombs to destroy a building. Moderate size, take out a room or two, maybe, something of that sort of level of explosion.'

'The posh guy is who?'

'Lord Hugh Wallace. Apparently, he used to be something amongst spies. I don't know what, but he's very manipulative. Mark told me to be wary of him, but trust everything he said. Mark gave me instructions for how to do the deals.'

'What instructions were those?'

'Doesn't matter now. They've come to kill me. They'll contact Mark in another way. I'm just a messenger. A messenger who obviously brought heat; therefore, they'll kill me.'

'What do you expect to get out of this?' asked Kirsten. 'Maybe if you talk enough, the people I work for might let you go somewhere.'

'What have I got to tell them? Mark contacts me. Well, that isn't happening anymore. I don't know where he is. The guys who meet me will go away and won't contact me again either. I don't know where your wheelchair man is, and as for Hugh Wallace, well, if I can find him, I'm sure you guys can.'

Kirsten watched the man for a while, and then she took up a seat in the corner. He was bound tightly, but Kirsten kept her gun with her and went into a sentry sleep. One where she'd be awake in an instant. One where any noise would make her react. When she woke up two hours later, her mind was made up. She placed a call from outside the shack to Justin Chivers.

She made her way back down into the underground shelter and looked around for more food. She'd put on a pot of potatoes, peas, and carrots and throw a little gravy in with it. There was a tin of beef as well that she heated afterwards and then combined the pots to make one almighty stew. She sat eating, taking her fill before feeding her captive. After she'd finished, she cleared up as best she could before sitting down in front of him again.

'Wallace,' she said. 'What is Wallace doing? What do you know about him?'

'He's part of them. He was doing the introductions, and the man in the wheelchair is probably more like a lieutenant. Someone to give the orders. He's a contact man. If he's been in the Service, he'll know how it'll work. He certainly knew how to work with me, how to do things on the quiet. I would suspect if he didn't, he'd be dead. He obviously blamed me for you watching us.'

'Correctly, because you were the one picked up. It was you I tailed from the hotel in Perth. For what it's worth, a tracker on your car. I watched you from a distance and would still be watching you if they hadn't come and found me. Yes, I agree with you, Danny. They're good, better than you, but then again, you rarely attract heat like me.'

The man looked up. He seemed wary, more than anything else. 'Always my problem,' he said, 'going for a good-looking woman. I should have seen the assassin coming.'

'I wouldn't beat yourself up over that one,' she said. 'It's a good honey trap. After all, you ordered a prostitute. It'd be better to know the women that you want to bed.'

'Wallace is funding. He's got a bit of money. When we talked, he seemed to be the money man. The other guy referred to him when we were talking about the budget. That's about all I know. On a timescale for the bomb, it was inside the next couple of months. We were talking loosely. We were going to firm up detail when their facilitator came in, told us to get out.'

'Do you have any clothes?' asked Danny. 'I'm just feeling a bit uncomfortable underneath this blanket.'

'I can take the blanket off if you want,' said Kirsten. 'You can feel truly uncomfortable. I have to be honest, Danny, I don't walk around with spare clothing for people. You get caught with your pants down, that's on you.'

There was a tap on the trapdoor above, and then a sound like the twitter of a robin. Why a robin would twitter at that time of night, who knew, but Kirsten knew it wasn't the one of the small, feathered kind.

'Don't open it,' said Danny. 'They may have tracked you.'

Kirsten undid the bolt on the trapdoor and tapped the trap

door twice with her hand. It was pulled open from above and Justin Chivers slid down the ladder into the shelter. He was dressed in a smart suit and tie, and gave her the once over and then looked at her captive.

'I never realised you were this kinky,' said Justin. 'I take it he's bound underneath that rug.'

'Hilarious. My friend Danny here went to bed with the wrong woman tonight. She tried to kill him. I just rescued him. He's hoping for a change of clothes. You haven't brought one with you, have you?'

'I'm afraid not,' said Justin. 'Has he said anything?'

'Danny's been telling me about the man he met in the wheelchair. Said the man in the wheelchair is probably a lieutenant or the like with these people ordering the bombs. The bombs are coming from Mark Lamb. Danny's running communications for him. He also said there was a Lord Hugh Wallace they met with.'

Justin twisted his head, staring at Kirsten.

'Oh, he knows him,' said Danny. 'He knows him.'

'Shush,' said Kirsten. 'What's the deal?'

'Upstairs,' said Justin, and climbed the ladder.

'Don't go away,' said Kirsten. 'We'll be back.' Her humour fell on deaf ears, and she climbed up into the shack before dropping the trap door.

'Lord Hugh Wallace—that changes things,' said Justin.

'You know him?'

'Lord Hugh Wallace is a legend in the Service. Of course, he's not known as Lord Hugh Wallace. Not that many people know who he is. Godfrey knows him. Godfrey and he used to work together. There was bad blood going on there as well.'

'It's Godfrey. Anna Hunt's got bad blood with Godfrey. You

have. I have. Everybody's got bad blood with Godfrey.'

'No. This is stronger than that.' Kirsten gave a stare at Justin.

'I know yours is as well. I know all that's happened with that, but understand me, this is worse. Yes, yours was all in the line of duty. Godfrey, over time, hasn't always been a model of the Service.'

'Well, he does things, doesn't he?' said Kirsten. 'His way of operating. Likes to play it loose sometimes. Very abrupt. Takes out his opponents.'

'No, no. He and Wallace fell out big time. Nobody quite knows why. Nobody quite knows what the tale of it was, but I'm telling you, it caused Wallace to leave the Service. You don't walk away from the Service. Not like that.'

'I walked away,' said Kirsten.

'No, you didn't. You were always still on tap. He was always coming back to you. It was always seen as a short-term thing, and then Godfrey used the situation after that to haul you back in. Sure, you're not working for us on a payroll, but you are on a mercenary front. You're still working for us. You're still looking to serve the country. Godfrey pulls the chain, yanks us, and we move,' said Justin. Kirsten wasn't thrilled about that comment.

'What else can you tell me about him?'

'Very little, very shadowy figure. However, I know he lives on an estate near Fashnacloich.'

'Am I meant to know where that is?' asked Kirsten.

'Near Appin. West Coast, down a bit.'

'I want you to take Danny into custody and hold him in the Service. I can't do it here. It's going to tie me down. I could be disappearing for a couple of days. A week, two weeks. If I've gone into cover, he'll be dead by the time I get back. Besides, he might tell you more.'

'If it's Wallace, I doubt he will. Did he tell you anything about Craig?' asked Justin

'I said nothing about Craig.'

'The wheelchair man. I'm a spy, but you don't need to be one to work that one out. I've also worked with you long enough to work out your disguised Service tells.'

'He thought Craig was like a lieutenant during their meetings,' said Kirsten. 'Keep Danny safe. Keep him out of the way and I'll go after Hugh Wallace. See where that leads me.'

'Are you wanting that blanket to stay here?' said Justin.

'Give him the blanket,' said Kirsten. 'You don't want to get stopped in a car with a nude man beside you. People will talk.'

'People talk about me all the time,' said Justin. 'Strangely enough, there are rumours about women. You've got to love it.'

Chapter 07

Fashnacloich was a trip down past Loch Ness and much further, continuing to the southwest. Close to Appin, deep in the countryside, Kirsten would take many small and seemingly insignificant roads to stop short of the estate of Lord Hugh Wallace. It wasn't grand and the surrounding fields were a mix of woodland and farming. At the centre was one quite simple estate house.

It looked like something built with Lego bricks because it was rectangular edged, with no fancy trims on the outside. The front door did indeed have two pillars, but it was almost as if they were obligatory. Something that came as one of the building pieces when you couldn't find something else. What Kirsten did note were the number of people that seemed to operate about the estate.

People working on estates rarely look like they can handle guns. They also don't look lean on the whole. In general professions, people are a mix. There are those who maybe have too much weight on, and those who have too little. They come in all shapes and sizes. Some work out, some will look muscly, some will look as if a trip to the shops would tire them out. They have a range of cars. They walk differently.

Certainly, they don't look like they're on patrol.

Having driven through most of the day, Kirsten spent the night watching the goings-on around the estate of Lord Hugh Wallace from a distance. There wasn't a lot of movement, but the cars that came were similar. High powered or else those which could tackle cross country. Big engines. There were no small cars.

In an average company's car park, yes, you'd get the big powerful beast that those who enjoy their cars want to have, but you got a lot of economical cars. Cars that people with less ego and a requirement to make their budgets fit drive all the time. Those sorts of cars didn't exist on the estate.

Kirsten felt the rain drip past her face as she watched. She didn't enjoy surveillance, but in fairness, at least out here in the country, the smell was good. The rain had brought it up, that fresh twang of the countryside. Wearing her rain gear, the water hadn't leaked through, and she was perfectly warm.

When morning broke, and the drizzle continued, she witnessed the arrival of Hugh Wallace. He pulled up in a Land Rover, stepped out, and was escorted by two guards on either side. It seemed unusual, but maybe she'd spooked them. After all, somebody was upsetting the apple cart. Maybe he was protecting himself.

By mid-morning, she felt she had enough, and she returned to her car to sleep, deciding that night she would break into the estate. She found a chip shop nearby Appin and enjoyed some chips while overlooking a loch, filling up with fuel as best she could. Tonight might be long, after all.

It was one in the morning when Kirsten exited her car some two miles away from the estate house, dressed entirely in black. Her hair tied up and tucked in underneath a balaclava, she felt ready to go. This was what she loved. The thrill and the excitement. Who'd have thought after all these years she'd be doing this?

Getting close to the estate house was easy and Kirsten made her way through fields, some ploughed, some not, and then through trees to the rear of the house. There was a large driveway from there, and she watched as a patrol occurred every twenty minutes. Whatever alarms were on obviously weren't activated at that time, and that would be her time to move.

She crouched behind a tree, waiting. She saw him move out, a guard, maybe in his twenties. He was built well, broad shoulders, big muscles, and she was sure he had a gun underneath his jacket. He walked with that step, probably ex-military, the timing so impeccable that Kirsten could almost hear a brass band playing in the background.

As he turned and walked along the back of the building, she stole out from behind the tree, following him at a distance. But she would need to get closer. Kirsten stopped at the corner and watched him as he looked left and right. She was out of view now, but she'd need to get close again, need to keep on his back. That's how she would enter the house.

She stayed at each corner of the house, three times, watching and waiting for him to turn the corner and then steal up behind him. After they'd nearly done a full circuit of the house and she got to the last corner, she hoped he would follow his normal habit.

He didn't look the same. There was no stare into the dark. He just wanted to get back inside. He'd done it the previous time, and this time he did it, too.

She sprinted up ever so quietly across the grass at the edge of the building, not wanting to go onto the driveway, always sticking to the soft grass. She watched him pull open the door, not even look around, and let the door close behind him. Kirsten ran as fast as she could and put the smallest of wedges in at the door. It looked like it had all but closed, but it hadn't. She waited twenty seconds. He should be clear, walked somewhere else by now.

Kirsten pulled open the door and stepped inside. There were lights on in a passageway. She could go left to a door that said 'Cleaner'. There were more doors to the right. Kirsten heard the click of the door behind her, but there was a small buzzer going off as well. She turned to the door beside her, found it to be open, and stepped inside.

It was the cleaners' room and on one side, had a rack full of cleaning products while there were mops and buckets on the floor. The roof was maybe seven feet up, extending another foot and a half above the door.

There had been a buzzer, Kirsten thought. She climbed the racking, but it wasn't that strong. She reached out with her hands across the gap and spread herself. Holding her weight by applying pressure through her feet and through her hands to opposite walls, Kirsten got herself up to the ceiling. She held herself there, tight.

There were footsteps in the corridor outside. She heard a door opening and closing and suspected it was someone checking the locking mechanism. The cleaner's door was then opened. Someone stared in. He looked around at the products, shaking his head, and closed the door again.

Kirsten waited. Her heart was beating fast, but she was breathing steady, trying to control the way she felt. After a couple of minutes, she dropped inside the cleaning cupboard and started looking at her watch. Someone would be back out on patrol soon, and she waited until she heard the door click.

It opened, and it shut. As soon as it did, Kirsten opened the cleaning door and stepped out into the hallway. She glanced up, but there was no security camera. Maybe that would come later. She didn't know. She stole along the corridor.

The first door she came to had nothing written on it and it was heavy and wooden. She listened closely. Somebody was on the other side, and somebody was snoring. Guard room maybe? She continued along the hall and found another door. She heard nothing on the other side. Slowly, she opened it, gun at the ready in case anyone would try to surprise her. When she opened it, it was dark, and she took a pocket flashlight out and shone it around the room. There were large sinks. This was clearly somewhere to get clean, some sort of scrub-down room.

Kirsten stepped back out into the corridor, checked the third door again, which had nothing behind it, and found a storeroom filled with drinks and tins of food. She then took the last door in the corridor. She stepped out into a large lobby and could see a door far off leading elsewhere, but there was also an enormous staircase. The stairs were marble underneath, she thought, and there was poor lighting. Maybe they patrolled indoors as well.

There was a red carpet running up the middle and at the top, the stairway went either way. For being so bland on the outside, the inside certainly looked grand. At the top of the stairs, she saw a large portrait and recognised it as the man she had seen through the binoculars in the conservatory. Lord Hugh Wallace certainly thought a lot of himself.

Somewhere he would have a study, or somewhere where he

kept everything of note about the operations he was involved in. It would be safely kept away from everyone else. There'd be some way for it to be locked. It would be a door that she couldn't open easily.

She ignored the staircase and instead went round towards the rear, finding another door. She walked through into another wood-panelled corridor, but each door along it was simple. *I could pick that lock*, she thought. This would need to be something special.

She followed the corridor on round, realised it was doubling back on itself. It was like a very simple maze heading into the middle. A pattern of right turns heading back to a central core. Yes, there were other doors coming off, but again, none of them were locked in any significant way, and then she came up against a solid steel door. There was a lock facing her. It was electronic, requiring a password.

This is it, she thought. *Bet it's not the only way into that room, either.* She traced her way back, back to the lobby with the large stairway. She crept up the red carpet and then suddenly had to steal herself up against the wall as somebody walked across the lobby at the foot of the stairs. They walked up, looking this way and that, and Kirsten crouched behind a marble banister.

Fortunately, the man turned the other way, but he'd be on a route. She followed him, walking slowly. The upper floor went round and came back on itself; one corridor with lots of rooms, easy to patrol, easy to find anyone. Stealing along, waiting for the man on patrol to disappear from in front of her, she listened carefully at each door until she heard loud snoring.

This door looked grander than the rest. Lord Hugh Wallace clearly thought something of himself, despite his skill to build a house on the outside that didn't look that impressive. Clearly, once you were inside, he wanted you to know he was important and above all others.

This must be his bedroom, she thought. The door wasn't locked, and she turned the handle ever so slowly before opening it quietly and sneaking in. A man slept in a grand four-poster bed and she could hear him snoring loudly. The covers were half back and lying beside him was a girl nearly half his age, covers straight across her legs while their top halves were laid bare.

Kirsten snuck around the room. Was there a different way to go down below? If there was, it would be here. It would be from his private abode. She scanned the walls, and she felt them slowly. There was nothing, absolutely nothing.

She heard a grunt from Hugh Wallace and crouched down in the dark. She saw him get up, and he made to grab for a dressing gown sitting on a chair beside him. Kirsten's eyes had been accustomed to the dark, and she saw his hand reaching for a light. Quickly, she slid in under the bed, silent in her movement.

The light came on, almost blinding to her eyes, and she had to half close them and let her eyes adjust slowly. She heard Wallace pad off. Maybe he needed the toilet. He was at that age when night time visits became normal.

Kirsten waited and, sure enough, a couple of minutes later, he came back into the bed. She heard some moans, some slurping from kisses, and after half an hour, the snoring began again. Kirsten emerged from under the bed.

Stealing back out, she edged carefully along corridors knowing that patrols would be coming. She made her way back downstairs, followed the loop round to stand in front of the metal door again. She looked up at the pad, but there was no way of knowing if you had to press numbers or letters or if there was a screen that would come up. Justin Chivers would be good at this, although she wasn't sure that even he could get it open. No, she'd have to do this some other way.

As Kirsten went to turn away, she could hear something. It was almost a whistling that you get from tinnitus. A noise that you might not think is there, or one you think you're imagining, but it was there. It was very high, and it was very persistent. Some sort of electronic device had been set off. Suddenly, the building seemed to come alive. She heard footsteps and Kirsten tore down the corridor. Then a loud alarm rang. All hell was breaking loose in the building, and she was stuck in the most inner loop of it. She'd have to be quick if she were going to get out alive.

Chapter 08

J ustin Chivers looked at the hand he was holding. Sure, he had two aces. He also had two fours and a seven on the table in front of him, and several notes. Justin would have to see the man next to him. His hand wasn't bad, two pairs. He'd rather have a full house, though, and so he threw in an extra note and took away a single card. It was passed to him and he looked at his cards.

Two aces, two fours now, and a three. It was two pairs. That was it. Not great. He looked at the man opposite him who had dealt the card. Playing amongst other people in the Service was difficult because most of them didn't have a tell. It was trained out of them. Justin threw a note in. After all, it was only money. Slowly, it went round and eventually there were only three of them to put their cards down. Somebody else had called early. The pot in the middle wasn't great. Justin put his two pairs on the table.

'I got you on that one,' said the man next to him, and he placed down his five cards. He had two aces as well and two sevens. The man next to him then placed down five cards, two aces, two eights, and a five. The fourth man at the table looked at the other three.

'I folded and I get the feeling that somebody's cheating here.'

There was a grin went round. Of course, somebody was cheating. When did you get six aces in a pack? Justin reached into the centre of the table, counted back the notes he put in, and put them in his pocket.

'I wish you guys would play properly,' he said. 'Someday we will and I'll take you to the cleaners.'

He stood up, stretched, and walked to the door of the living room. He opened it and made his way up the stairs. It was a detached house in Inverness on the outskirts of town and on a new estate. Two of the men in the house lived there permanently, posing as a couple. Justin laughed because neither of them were of that persuasion. Daniel was standing up on the landing, looking out of the window. The light was off and it would've been hard to see him from outside.

'Anything?' asked Justin.

'Nothing. Well, actually, two cars have gone past in the last ten minutes.'

'Two cars? You think it was two different cars?'

'Yes, two different ones.'

'How many people in them?' asked Justin.

'Three in the first, four in the second. Looked like people coming back from a night out. Some of them seemed to be quite dressed up.'

Justin nodded and then walked over to one of the bedroom doors. He pushed it open and inside, there was a small comfortable bed on which lay Danny Kyle. He was wearing clothes now, but a duvet was around him and he was sleeping silently.

Justin exited the bedroom, nodded over to Daniel, and made his way downstairs again. For the next twenty minutes, he drank a cup of coffee that had been made for him by one of the other men. Once he'd finished, he felt the urge to be on the move.

He hated this. He was stuck in a house guarding Danny Kyle, and he needed to wait there until Godfrey came to pick him up. That was the other thing that was bothering him. Godfrey was coming personally. It involved Kirsten, but Kirsten had done her job. Kirsten was bringing someone in and had even got the man to talk. The next stage would be to put him in front of some decent interrogators from the Service. There was no need for Godfrey to come, and yet he was, and at pace.

Justin yawned. He decided he was going to take a walk. Not far away. He'd still be within sight of the house, and it wasn't always a bad idea to go out and scan the land around, make sure nothing was going on. You can only see so much from the house.

He needed to get his coat from upstairs and so stepped back out of the lounge and went to the stairs. As he did so, the front door of the house suddenly blew open.

It had been hit with something. He didn't know if it was a small missile, but he saw the door fly past him down the hallway beside the stairs. Justin was thrown onto the stairs, his shoulder taking the full brunt of hitting the wooden staircase. There was a yell and a scream, but Justin was already getting himself back up on his feet to run up the stairs. There were cries from down below, cries from up above, and Justin sprinted straight for Danny Kyle's room.

'Get up,' shouted Justin, as he burst through the door of the room. He threw back the covers and Danny Kyle's eyes opened. He'd been awoken by the blast of the door being blown in, but he was still groggy. 'What's up?'

'We've got to go. We've got to go.'

'I'll get my shoes.'

'No,' said Justin. 'We go.'

He grabbed the man's wrist, dragging him towards the bedroom door. Justin quickly peered out. His colleague, Daniel, should have been at the window at the top covering the stairs, and he saw him being shot in the head. The man hit the back wall, blood splattered everywhere, and he tumbled to the ground.

'*Damn it*, thought Justin, drawing his weapon out from inside his jacket. 'You get behind me, you stay right behind me. Do not step away. Do not run elsewhere,' said Justin to Danny Kyle. 'I will get you out of here. You need to trust me.'

Danny Kyle nodded and obediently stepped in behind Justin. Justin peered once, twice, out of the door and shots rang past his head. He turned, 'Stay here!'

Justin rolled out of the door, across to the top of the stairs, and as he came up, he looked down and saw the figure who had fired previously. Justin fired two shots in quick succession. The man bounced back into the panel beside the front door and then collapsed. Justin heard footsteps and jumped up, peering over the banister to see another man coming. He fired two more shots straight into his head.

He then saw more people coming through the front door. Quickly, he stepped back into the bedroom where Danny Kyle was. He looked around. There was an office bureau in the bedroom. He reached over and pulled the front end of it away from the wall. 'Give me a hand,' he shouted.

Together, the two then got behind the bureau and started pushing it towards the door of the bedroom.

'We need to lock the door, then put this up against it,' said

Danny.

'No,' said Justin. Together they rammed the bureau towards the open door where it then sailed out and onto the wooden floor of the upper landing. It slid across to the top of the stairs. In its ultimate position, no one could get to the bedroom without clambering over the top of it. Justin crouched down, telling Danny to get inside the room and then all the way to the back wall. He did so. When Justin looked back to see one attacker hurdling the top step and up onto the bureau, he fired twice and the man's body lay on top of the bureau. He watched the blood drip, his heart pounding.

Justin breathed deeply. An eerie silence was filling the house. He turned and looked around the bedroom he was in. There was a window at the back. The garage was beneath it.

'Danny, over here. Now!'

Danny Kyle ran over to him and crouched down. Where Justin was, someone would have to be looking straight into the window to have seen him. If he were to the right-hand side from where Justin was looking, he could be out of Justin's view and still be looking into the bedroom at the far wall. That's where Danny was. Justin kept flicking his head back and forward. He was surrounded. A face appeared at the window, raising a gun, and Justin fired twice. He heard footsteps on the stairs.

They're coming for us, he thought. *They're coming straight in, pincer.*

'Danny, window, now, go.'

Justin stood up, stepped out, and fired several times down the stairs. He caught someone, he was sure of it. Hearing shots firing back, he crouched down again, getting behind the bureau. He reached up above it and pushed the body that was

64

there, hearing it bounce down the stairs. With that, he turned and fled back to the bedroom.

Danny was just getting through the window, and Justin jumped up behind him. There was no one on the garage roof. It had been a risk, and he wasn't sure if it would work, but he had to move fast.

Danny tumbled out the window, shouting for a moment as he cut himself on the glass. Justin saw the body lying beneath the window, hurdled up onto the window ledge from the bedroom and out onto the roof of the garage.

'Tight into the wall,' he said to Danny. He stole in front of him, tucked himself in, looked down, and saw a car parked in the driveway. He turned, looking back at Danny, and saw a head pop out of the bedroom window.

'Down,' he blurted. Danny ducked, and Justin fired two shots into the head. He didn't wait to see the impact. He knew he had hit his target. Instead, he reached, grabbed Danny, and threw him off the garage roof and onto the car below.

Justin followed him down, landing on the bonnet, rolling off to one side behind the car. He went to grab Danny off the top of the roof, pulling him, but someone had stepped out of the front door of the house. There were two sickening thuds into Danny's body as Justin pulled him down. Danny's body collapsed down beside Justin. He saw the man was still breathing, but he'd been shot in the stomach and the chest. Blood was seeping.

'We can still get you in,' he said. 'Come on.'

He pulled him behind the car, but two men were running out of the house now. Justin left Danny, stepped behind the car, tight to the rear end of it, and shot one man over the top. The man shot back, causing Justin to duck. When Justin reared up again, he saw that the second man had rounded the front of the car. There were two shots being pumped into Danny.

All Justin could do was fire back, taking the man at the front of the car first. He rebounded back into the garage door, causing it to thud and ring out through the night. Blood ran across the white door. Before the man had even fallen, Justin had put another two bullets into his colleague on the other side of the car.

Justin stepped forward, looking down at Danny. Half the face wasn't there. There was no movement from the body. Justin flung open the car door, climbed in, and pulled the keys out of his pocket. He started the car, reversed incredibly quickly, spinning out of the drive. There was a car coming the other way that sounded its horn at him. It rode the curb beside him, but Justin didn't care. He put the foot down, driving off through the estate.

Damn it, he thought. *Damn it.*

He tried to breathe easy. Tried to think about what was going on. They'd been attacked in a safe house. Someone had got where they were. He hadn't been followed. He was too good for that. Justin knew how to operate, and he had not been followed. Somebody had come to the place knowing where it was. A leak from inside. It must have come from inside. It must have.

Suddenly, it clicked with Justin. Godfrey was coming. Godfrey would be on his way. He reached in to his pocket and grabbed his mobile phone, dialling Godfrey's number. What if it was overheard? What would it matter now?

'This is Godfrey,' said a voice on the other end.

'Chivers. Been compromised. The man we were holding is dead. I repeat. Man we're holding is dead. Compromised, been attacked. Get out, get away now.'

There was no response, just a phone going dead. Godfrey may not have been that far away for all Justin knew.

Chivers reached the edge of the estate looking to drive onto a main road, when the car in front of him suddenly pulled over. It jerked to a halt. For a moment, Justin thought he'd seen a flash from inside. Then he saw a tall, thin man stepping out of the car.

He had been in the rear, and Justin watched him open the front door and look inside. The man was holding a gun. Justin spun the car round and parked it up in front of the other car that had stopped. He rolled down the window as the thin man turned and pointed a gun at him.

'Inside,' said Justin. 'Inside.'

Godfrey ran over to him, opened up the passenger door, and jumped in. 'Time to go,' said Godfrey.

'Where?'

'You got any of your own near here?'

He was referring to hideaways. There were the ones used by the Service, but there were others known only to operatives. Similar to Kirsten's shack.

'Yes,' said Chivers, 'but it won't be the most comfortable.'

'The hell with comfort. They're all through us, Chivers. They're throughout us. We trust no one.'

Chapter 09

Kirsten knew she was trapped. The circling corridor that led into the middle of the building meant she would struggle to get back out. They would just simply keep flooding it with people and she'd have to shoot her way past all of them. Kirsten had every belief in her prowess with a weapon. But everyone could be outmatched with firepower.

As the thought raced through her head, a door opened and a man with a gun ran out of one room. Kirsten didn't hesitate, shooting him with her silent weapon and watching him tumble to the ground. She could keep going round and round, she thought. At some point, they'd block her off. Even then, she'd still have to figure another way out.

The windows would be better. If she could get out through a window, make her escape that way. She stopped, opened the door into a room, and found it to be a sleeping quarter. A man was already halfway out of bed, reaching for his gun. Kirsten strode over and kicked him hard off the wall. As he bounced back, she manoeuvred her arm around his neck and snapped it. He crumpled to the ground.

There are no windows, she thought suddenly. *Where are the windows?* There was, however, a lock on the door. Kirsten strode forward, turned the key in the lock, and then turned to look around the room. There was the bed, there was a desk with a computer on it, a chair as well. There was a wardrobe, too.

Kirsten opened the door of the wardrobe and began scanning through the clothes therein. There were several jackets, a few of them were Barbour green. Of course, everyone here would have to look like they were farmhand. Someone to do with the estate. Even the man that had stepped out of the room had been dressed casually.

Kirsten grabbed one of the Barbour coats and put it on over her own. She had a small rucksack on her back. From the back, it would look like she had some type of hunch, but from the front, she'd get away with it. Her trousers were black, as were her boots. The Barbour jacket might just give her a moment. It could put a hesitation in people's minds.

There came a knock at the door. Someone tried to open it.

'Coming,' said Kirsten, in as gruff a voice as she could manage. She unlocked the door, opened it to find a man standing there. He looked very shocked to see her face, and she grabbed him, pulling him into the room and driving a knee up into his midriff. As he fell to the floor, she closed the door behind her, locking it once again.

He turned with a gun, and she swatted it from his hand with a swipe of her foot. As she went forward for him, he pitched at her, driving her backwards into the door. She hit it with a thud, and he scrambled, running over to the far corner of the room. Once there, he hit a panel which slid back.

Kirsten was up on her feet now, but before the man could make his way through the open hatchway, she shot him straight through the head. A second bullet made sure.

She ran over and pulled the body out of the way. She then shoved the bed up against the door and stepped inside the strange compartment that had been opened for her.

Once inside the hatchway, Kirsten found herself in a tight passageway. It had steps going up, and she climbed them slowly. The entire passageway was lit, but with the emergency lighting one would expect after a power cut. Slowly she climbed, listening as best she could to the surrounding walls. Where she would come out, she didn't know, but someone would come looking for the man who banged on her door. They would come up behind her. Forward was the only way.

The passageway turned left, still climbing, and then right. She realised she must be up a floor. It then went flat, and she walked along it before coming to the end. She could see the panel that would slip aside in front of her. Rather than pressing it, she listened carefully.

There was no noise from the room. Nothing to say that anyone was inside. She pressed the button that slid the panel back and looked into a dark room. She shone a torch around it. It was a small dining room with a table at the centre. At the most, you could fit six around it. Maybe this was his personal dining area. Maybe this is where Lord Hugh would eat.

Closing the panel behind her, she quietly stole around the room. There was a window on the far side and she looked out onto grounds where men were gathered outside. There was a conference going on, clearly deciding if she'd left the house or not. They didn't even know it was a her, specifically. Were they worried it was a false alarm? Did they know someone was about?

Kirsten sat down in one of the large chairs at the table, trying to gather her thoughts for a moment. Downstairs, she had a room she couldn't get into. She needed to be in there. She didn't have the likes of Justin Chivers who could break in past that code to gain access to the electrics. On her own, those skills were lacking.

She could blow the door, but it would make so much noise. Of course, she was assuming she could blow the door. She did not know how thick it was, no idea of what prevented her from getting into that room. Ideally, she wanted the door to be opened for her.

Always think the easiest thing. If you're going to do something, what would make it easiest for you? Someone opening the door for her would be the easiest way. She couldn't very well walk up and ask Lord Hugh. She doubted she could kidnap him, not from this place. Get a hold of him and threaten to go in. Seeing how quick they were to kill people they were working with, maybe they'd just kill him.

Taking a hostage was never a good idea unless you were sure that the other people cared about that hostage. She knew too little to be sure of that. *Maybe*, she thought, *Just maybe*.

Kirsten looked out of the window again and counted the number of men out there. Then she stole over to the main door of the dining room. She listened and then opened it carefully, peering outside. She could see no one. There was a lot of commotion from downstairs.

She stepped out onto the upper landing. Turning right, then taking a few quick steps, she could look out on the stairs. No one was guarding them. Clearly, they'd found the dead body down below. They'd sent somebody in after her. Someone else would come to break down that door. They must have thought she was trapped. At some point, they'd realise she

71

might go up the passage. Of course, they needed to be quick.

Instead of going down the large stairway with the red carpet, she headed back and went round the loop to where the main bedroom of Lord Hugh was. There'd be nobody inside there now except—

Kirsten opened the door of his bedroom and she saw a figure lying spread out on top of the bed. It hadn't turned over. Maybe she was in half a stupor, sleeping. Kirsten walked over quietly and then placed her gun on the back of the woman's neck.

'Get up,' she said. The woman shook and slowly she edged away off the bed and stood naked before Kirsten. 'Go over to where you keep your dressing gown and put it on,' said Kirsten. 'Do anything outside of what I tell you and I will kill you.'

The woman walked over, slipped on a dressing gown, and then stood looking at Kirsten. Kirsten guessed the woman could have been only in her early twenties, an escort at best, maybe an outright prostitute, but someone just caught up in the action.

'If you do as I say, I will not kill you,' said Kirsten. 'Deviate from what I say in the slightest detail and I will despatch you immediately. In a few minutes, you're going to walk out of here and run down that red carpet screaming. You're going to tell everyone that someone entered the room and left through the window.'

Kirsten eased away to the window and looked out. There was no one there.

'Tell them to look south because that's where I went, south of here. Okay?'

Kirsten took off its fastenings, ready to swing it out. It was a long drop, but she had a small grappling hook and rope in her backpack. She took those out, ready to go. She looked over at the woman.

'Take some advice from me, find a different job. If you are going to do this job, don't take bookings from people like this. They're just not trustworthy, just not worth it. Now get out there and make sure you scream all the way.'

Kirsten watched the woman run for the door, pull it open and scream as loud as she could. By the time she would have reached the enormous staircase, Kirsten would be down the outside of the wall. She dropped the grappling line, holding till she reached the bottom. Then she quickly unhinged the grappling hook, letting it fall, picking it up and putting it in her backpack.

From there, she ran as hard as she could. At the edge of where the main estate house was, there was a large garage. During the days of observation, Kirsten had seen some cars come and go and decided that this would be a good place to plunder. She grabbed a motorbike from inside, started it and drove out, whipping her way into the darkness.

She didn't head for the main road, but across a field. As she did so, she heard shouts behind her, shots being fired in her direction. There was then a shout at those who had fired, people told to get other transport and to follow.

Kirsten drove through a hedge, finding the smallest gap, widening it somewhat. She then tore across a muddy field, setting up good tracks all the way, headed towards a wooded area. Once inside the wood, she drove along a path briefly and then turned off, leaving the motorbike some distance off the path in the undergrowth.

She turned back, running as hard as she could, at right angles to the house. From where she was, Kirsten could see the pursuers in the distance coming now with lights and torches. She ran perpendicular to them until she believed she was well clear, delighted they were coming after her. She then turned and cut back, heading directly for the house.

As she sprinted through the woods and got to the fence that surrounded the estate area, she could see Lord Hugh outside. That was where she wanted him. He was giving instructions, telling everyone where to go, what to do. Then he turned and headed for the rear of the house. Kirsten was over the fence in the dark, running up to the side next to the rear of the house.

When she could see no one, she sprinted across and got to juke around the corner to see Lord Hugh arrive at the rear door and open it. She pursued. He may have been the only one in the house, and she hoped so, because he would go to one place. The house had been compromised, and he didn't know exactly where she'd been.

Had she been in that room? Were there other ways to access that room other than the front door, the main one that she couldn't bypass?

As she entered the rear door, Hugh was going through the door at the end of the corridor. Kirsten sprinted up behind him as quietly as she could. Once she reached that door, she counted briefly, then opened it. She saw Hugh making his way down the corridor, the one that kept turning at right angles, moving nearer and nearer to the middle of the house. She walked along, seeing him step over the dead body of the man she'd shot earlier.

Quickly and calmly, Lord Hugh made his way round to the middle of the house. Kirsten followed him, as quiet as anything. When he got to the door, she watched as he pressed several letters and numbers on a screen. The main door slid back, as did a second one, and Hugh walked in.

Kirsten followed him, gun out, pointed right at the back of his head. She stole in behind him quickly, ghost walking, able to move off to the right before Hugh turned to the left. He sat down in a seat in front of a computer screen, tapped in a password, unaware that Kirsten was even behind him. But she'd need to do more than that.

Quickly, she looked around her. There was a desk in the rear with a chair in front of it. If she was quick and quiet, she'd get in there. Kirsten moved over and delicately moved the chair out of the way. She crawled into the space under the desk and reached forward with her hands, moving the chair back.

She was soundless, as she'd been taught in her training. Lord Hugh checked files on the computer, then looked around the room. The room wasn't brightly lit, most of the lighting coming from screens and dials, equipment around it. There were some low-level lights on the walls, and in the gloom, he completely failed to see Kirsten sitting with a gun in front of her, just in case he noticed her.

Soon, he stood up from the desk and walked off, returning to the corridor to see how the search for Kirsten was going. At least, that was what she presumed. The door slammed shut. Kirsten waited. She'd give it five minutes in case he came back and then she'd move the chair away and she'd find out what she had in here. She was trapped inside, but he'd given her what she wanted, access to the room at the heart of his estate. The one where he was hiding something. All she had to do now was find out what.

Chapter 10

Godfrey was a quiet passenger as Justin Chivers drove out of Inverness and south towards Aviemore. Justin had a safe house there, a small flat, which he maintained. He had picked it up in the time he had worked in the north, and now, like always, he felt it was good to keep places.

It had been done at his own expense. He hadn't even taken the money from the Service for it. Maybe the money he'd spent on acquiring it had come from not the best of sources, but he was owed a bit. After all, they put his life in danger too often.

He drove down to Aviemore and stopped in the centre of the town. The hour was late, and he looked across at Godfrey.

'I think it's wise that we go separately. You need to go to your place and I to mine.'

'Do you not trust me?' asked Godfrey.

'Now is not a time to trust people. I trust no one. You can contact me, though. That won't be a problem. Take the car. It's one of the Service one's anyway, so it might be monitored. Ditch it somewhere. Get yourself something else from somebody you trust. Is there anyone you trust?'

'Brenda,' said Godfrey.

'Your bodyguard?'

'Yes, Brenda,' said Godfrey. 'She's taken a bullet for me before. I trust Brenda to look after me. That's where I'll go. But you're right, Mr Chivers. It's time to batten down the hatches. They're all over us. I need to know who, and I need to know why. If you hear from Kirsten, do pass on my regards, and ask for an update. I shall push all the channels. Take care of yourself, Mr Chivers. I don't think you're one of the bad guys. If you are, you're pulling out a heck of a story just to keep your cover.'

Justin stepped out of the car, leaving the keys inside. He walked off in the wrong direction in Aviemore and waited until Godfrey had departed before turning back. He walked across quiet residential streets until he came to the flat he owned. On reaching, he pressed the access code, climbed the stairs to the top-floor. He set the key guard code, got the front door key, opened it, and stepped into his flat.

Slowly, he walked around and spent the next ten minutes checking everything. The phone was intact. Didn't look like it had been picked up. Nothing seemed to be out of place. If somebody had gone through here, they'd done a fantastic job of it.

Justin sighed, made his way to the bathroom, and took his clothes off for a shower. When he emerged half an hour later, he grabbed his dressing gown and made himself a meal. He picked out some tinned potatoes, some tinned carrots, before pouring in some water. From the freezer, he extracted some meat that had been there less than two weeks. He threw it in the microwave, chopped an onion up and threw it in as well.

Next, Justin took a stock cube, placed it inside the pot,

and allowed the water to mix with it. Soon everything was bubbling over. He gave it a taste.

It needs some Worcester sauce, he thought. Reaching over to the fridge, he opened the door, took the Worcester sauce from inside, and dropped a little into the pot. He stared at it, wondering about Godfrey's words. He then took the Worcester sauce and placed it back on the top rack of the fridge.

It was then he stopped. For a moment, he halted and then closed the fridge door. On the inside of the door was something small and round, something that hadn't been there before. Carefully, he opened the fridge again, taking out the Worcester sauce bottle, his eyes flicking over to the spot where he thought he had seen the small round lens. It was small, but it was there.

Justin closed the door of the fridge again. He stared at the stew carefully before opening the fridge one more time and checking what he'd seen. The Worcester sauce bottle was put back, and the door was closed.

Justin had got this flat on his own. He'd got it outside of the Service. The woman who came and cleaned it hadn't come from the Service. He spoke to her directly and only to her. She didn't even know his real name. The money that paid for what she did came from a different account. They could not have known about this safe house unless he was being tailed.

Had somebody followed him? Had somebody been checking on him all this time? This was no random coup. Not something that was unplanned, amateurishly done. This was detailed. Somebody was at the core of this. Lord Hugh?

He was good, but this was Godfrey level. Was Godfrey having a clear-out by strange means? Justin Chivers was bemused, and it was not something that he was used to. Chivers could see the plans. Chivers could see the way people thought. It was what kept him alive. It's what kept him ahead. But now, as he stood in a dressing gown stirring stew, he realised that he'd been being watched. Safe houses were no longer safe. If they could find this one, they could have found any of them. Somebody had been tailing him, and he didn't even know.

As his stew continued to simmer, Justin went and got changed, taking clothes from the wardrobe. He didn't keep an extensive selection here, but he had a casual set. Normally, he liked a shirt and tie, but now he dressed in black jeans, a black T-shirt, and a leather jacket. He put boots on as well. Pouring himself some of the stew, he stood at the window with the lights out in the flat, staring.

He couldn't see anybody watching at the moment. Was that the point? He didn't need to. He had the camera. They wanted to know where he was. At some point, he would open the fridge. If he opened the fridge door, he bet the camera was triggered to come on, triggered to alert and to show if it was him. They would need to know it was him.

If you kept a safe house secret from everyone else, somebody still had to maintain it. If it wasn't you, the last thing you wanted to do was to bring an innocent into the situation. It wouldn't help your cause. It would just cause a problem if they got caught in the crossfire.

Suitably dressed and also replenished with the stew he had just eaten, Justin packed a small bag, securing some arms he had in the house. He then left the building, disappearing out into the night and walked the streets towards the middle of Aviemore. Once there, he cut left and worked his way back to the flat, but this time clambering through gardens, keeping off the street.

If someone had been merely watching him, he wanted to make sure they thought he had left, but that wasn't what he suspected. He suspected they were looking for him to be in, and they may come for him.

It was about half an hour since he left the house, and he was sitting in a garden across the road from the flat. The rain fell, but Justin was patiently sitting on his bottom inside a hedge, watching. Sure, it'd be a pain to get back out, and he'd have to do it quietly, but the rain would help with that. He was more keen to see if anybody arrived.

If I was eating, what would I do? Give me an hour. Give me an hour and a half. Make sure I'd gone to bed. He'd left the lights off in the flat now, so when they turned up they would think that. Surely someone would turn up.

It was nearly five in the morning when a van pulled up outside the flat. Justin couldn't see the far side of it, but he heard a door slide open and people jump out. They were quiet, and he saw the door of the flat being opened, people going up the stairs.

Quietly he emerged from the hedge, making a beeline across and keeping out of the mirror view of the van. He approached the passenger door. He didn't have a quick look. Instead, he opened it suddenly, gun in front of him, silencer on, and shot the man sitting in the driver's seat. Quickly, he pulled the man towards him, and clambered over his body in the passenger seat, placing himself into the driver's seat. If anyone looked down, they'd see a figure there. Justin made sure that the light was off in the cabin, so they couldn't tell who it was.

He watched the light going on in his flat, saw people moving about, searching. It took them about ten minutes before someone looked down from the window towards the van. They gave a single nod with their thumb pointed down. Justin put an acknowledging hand out the window, before four men who had climbed out from the van came back down and emerged out of the front door of the flats.

They came up towards the van, whose door was still pulled back. Each one clambered inside of it, then slapped the front, and Justin heard the door close behind him. He drove off, heading out of Aviemore, south into the back of nowhere. Once he disappeared further down the road, he cut off, heading up into hills and then down a track away from the main road.

He stopped, climbed out of the front, weapon in hand. He banged on the door and it was pulled back. The first man was shot in the face. The next two he was able to tap in the head. He only caught the last one in the shoulder. It took him a moment to tag him again. He searched them, every one, producing his phone and taking photographs. He had an idea about them. Thought he had seen one before.

Justin left the van where it was, but closed the door. Somebody would find it at some point. He needed to be out of there.

He walked along until he reached one of the main roads. Then he put a phone call in for a taxi. He had it take him back to Aviemore, where he walked in to the front desk of a hotel asking if there were any rooms available. He was told there were, and he booked in for the next couple of days.

Justin made himself a cup of coffee with the packet in the hotel room. He sat down at the small wooden desk, taking his phone out and tapped into the Service connection. Through it, he started scanning personnel files, doing it highly random fashion.

Godfrey had been wanting people to come in and be interviewed, so there was nothing unusual about what he was doing. It took him about half an hour, but soon Justin was sitting with the realisation that the four men he had just killed were all Service. More than that, they were long-term Service, each having served over ten years. He lay down on the bed, wondering to himself what was going on.

Was it Godfrey? Was he tearing the place inside out for some reason? It was a terrifying thought. The idea that Godfrey had found something and was checking through everyone. But the more terrifying thought was somebody had infiltrated the Service, and Godfrey didn't know. Somebody had recruited people, and Godfrey didn't know. He was the master spy.

Justin needed to go to ground. He needed to keep himself away for now. Don't talk to too many people. *Who did he trust? Did he trust Godfrey? Had that been a ploy tonight? Had Godfrey just been backing himself? But if so, why would he come for him? Why would Godfrey want Danny Kyle killed, and in such a bizarre fashion? It'd be easier to take him into custody and make him disappear. That would've been a Godfrey trick if it was needed.* No, something was wrong. Something wasn't right, but in the meantime, Godfrey had a rather large mark against his name.

What about Anna Hunt? Anna Hunt, behind it all, was an idealist. Anna Hunt wanted the Service to work. If Anna Hunt thought it was compromised, she could instigate something like this. She had the wit, but he trusted Anna, didn't he? He'd always trusted Anna.

She'd been good to him, but being good to people doesn't mean you trusted them. Didn't mean they always came out on your side. She was strong enough to do the right thing, even if it meant having to get rid of someone like Justin. He couldn't see it though. Why?

Kirsten? He thought he trusted Kirsten, but she'd been on the outside. Her man was possibly involved in this. Craig had been a good guy, but he'd changed at that fateful time when Justin had inadvertently blown the legs off him while trying to rescue him.

Justin felt his hands shake. During his career, he'd been on top of things. He'd seen what was coming. Right now, he was struggling to know who his friends were, who any of his friends were.

Chapter 11

It wasn't as bad as sitting in total darkness waiting for someone to come back at an unknown time, but not that far off, either. Sure, there was some light as various buttons on panels were still glowing. The whir of machinery threatened to keep Kirsten awake anyway, even if she hadn't intended to be. Descending into that sentry sleep, she listened carefully with eyes closed. She'd be awake in an instant if anything happened.

She laughed at how they must be scouring the countryside now, looking for her. Doubling back had been clever. It was the last place they'd think to look, especially after Hugh Wallace had returned. He had entered the main room of the building, believing everything was okay.

As she sat in the dim light, Kirsten checked through her backpack and her outfit. She ditched the stolen Barbour jacket. The other jacket she had on was a new one and there were several modifications from the previous ones. The more she got into the spy business, the more she wanted escape routes. Things she could use. Within this one were several throwing knives, small implements sewn into the jacket, but also what she liked to call a kite.

Sewn up the inside of the sleeves and down the side of the waist was a run of material. When ripped open, it produced an expansive material that turned her into a human kite. Could she jump off a mountain and glide down? Well, it wasn't as good as those suits, but it would certainly provide a large air brake if she jumped from a height. The trouble was, once it was deployed out of the jacket, it stayed out of the jacket. But it was an emergency backup for her.

She'd been in enough scrapes in this business to know that you needed every advantage. Everything had to be at hand, and right now, with the world tumbling, she felt comforted by the gear she had.

Kirsten climbed out from where she was and took photos of everything. There were plans, but the plans were coded. Still, she took photographs of them, anyway. Slowly she walked around the room, feeling every panel, seeing if there was any other way to get into the room. Down near the floor was a ventilation panel. Of course, with the equipment in here, the heat would need to escape. You couldn't lock it in completely.

Kirsten pulled at the panel, but it didn't budge. She reached inside her backpack, pulling out a small screwdriver that took the corners from the panel, kicking off the fascia. Kirsten looked inside. It was tight, but she could climb up there. She couldn't have her backpack on. The backpack would need to either go before or after her, but she could get up there.

However, she wasn't just here to photograph things and get out. She wanted to talk to Lord Hugh, wanted to find out from him what was going on. Craig had been with him. He had brought Craig in the wheelchair. Craig would need somebody to take him about. It wasn't as if he could simply walk anywhere, but why was he so important to them? A paraplegic.

He couldn't be half the operative he was before, but he had a mind, thought Kirsten. *Was his mind what they wanted? Why was he doing this? I get he was injured. I get he is angry at what had happened to him, but they paid for doctors. The Service had done right by him to a large degree.*

For all his mental fortitude, it seemed that Craig couldn't handle losing the lower half of his legs. She'd always thought he was stronger than that, but then again, she'd never been through an amputation. Just how did it get to you? How much did it take something from you?

She remembered lying in bed with Craig not long after he'd come back to the flat. She had come in that evening, determined to rekindle their relationship, determined to regain the physical side that was lost in Zante. It was when she was on top of him she saw his anger. In what should have been a perfect moment, the union of the pair of them, all she saw was hate; hate because he couldn't love her. He couldn't be the dominant lover anymore. He just couldn't.

It was so unfair. Kirsten loved him. She would continue to love him. That parts of him were missing wouldn't have stopped her loving him. She'd have done anything to make the union work, but he just hated himself. To not stand the skin that you're in was a hell that Kirsten was struggling to come to terms with.

Kirsten screwed the vent back on and then took a moment to sit back on the desk and breathe slowly. She found herself becoming agitated. She was thinking too deeply about Craig, and it would gnaw at her judgment when she would need it.

Kirsten heard the door slide to one side before she heard anything from outside. Maybe there was a soundproof dome around the room. Maybe it was thoroughly isolated. Whatever the case, she hadn't heard Lord Hugh approach, but when the door slid back, she raced underneath the table.

Kirsten watched him as he made his way towards the main desk. The computer was switched on. The door that protected the room slid back. He was locked inside. Lord Hugh was alone, or so he thought. She watched him log into the computer, but he didn't call anyone. He didn't link through to anyone. He was simply reading text off the screen.

Slowly, Kirsten unravelled herself from underneath the table and crept up behind him. She took out one of the small knives located inside her jacket and carefully she put it up to his throat. Pressing it in, she drew a fleck of blood, but not enough to damage permanently. His body flinched, and then he seemed to settle.

'Awful lot going on for an ex-Serviceman,' said Kirsten. 'Do you want to fill me in on what's happening?'

He didn't seem to move for a moment, and then she heard him crunch something. As she held his neck, he foamed at the mouth. His body jerked. Kirsten stepped away and watched as the man fell across his desk down to the floor, but a trailing hand caught a button.

Suddenly, alarms were blaring inside the room. Maybe they were blaring outside, too. Lord Hugh was fitting on the floor and then went strangely silent.

The room was at the centre of a twisting corridor, one that folded in on itself. Kirsten knew that trying to get back out of that door would involve her in probably the bloodiest firefight she'd ever had. She doubted she'd survive it.

Reaching inside her backpack, she ran over to the grill, clutching the facia for the vent, unscrewing it again, and leaving it on the floor. She grabbed her bag, pushing it up the vent, and then squeezed herself in. Her shoulders rubbed tightly, but she drove herself on up. The bag was up above her and she had to keep her hands held up too, such was the tightness. With her elbows touching the side, she pulled herself up, using her knees from below. Her feet were scrambling for purchase. She'd have to be quick. They'd be coming.

As she climbed, she wondered what sort of hold these people had on the likes of Lord Hugh. He hadn't even tried, hadn't even begun. Kirsten's bag suddenly hit something above. It was another grill. Bracing herself with her knees in the vent, she allowed the bag to drop onto her head. She unzipped part of it and reached in, fumbling until she found a small cylindrical object.

Taking it out, she made sure it was pointed the right way before she accidentally killed herself. Then she pressed a button and a burning torch, with an incredibly fiery flame, emerged from the other side. She'd only have enough fuel in the system for about three minutes, and so she quickly attacked the vent above her.

The grill was burnt through and, pushing her bag up, she knocked out enough of a hole. She threw the bag out through it and pulled herself up, squeezing through the gap. As she cleared the vent, she heard the first shot ricochet up it. Kirsten dropped to the roof of the building she was on.

The estate house was not the most elegant, but it had a chimney high above everything else. Kirsten reckoned it was maybe a fifty-feet drop to the ground below. She guessed they would be outside now, but she stole over to the edge of the building. Sure enough, out they came, weapons pointed up towards the sky. The morning was here and red soaked the horizon like burning clouds.

A sailor's warning, she thought. *Trouble was ahead; a very apt way to die*, but she wouldn't die today. She took off her jacket and began ripping up the side of it, and underneath the arms. Kirsten found the material and pulled it out on either side, producing a large kite. There'd be no proper structure to it yet. Only when she leapt would the wind take the sails under her and lift her. Or at least hopefully slow her from hitting the ground.

Kirsten carefully walked to the edge of the estate house. There was a fence further out and around, but not that high. The trouble was, it would slow her up while everyone was chasing her. She reached inside her bag, looked down, and collected a couple of tiny explosives. She primed them and went over to the northern side of the building. There was a good escape route there if you could get to the ground. Maybe they'd think she would go that way. It was time to find out.

She primed some devices, threw them off the edge, and stepped back. Carefully, she slung her backpack around her, made sure that the kite material was pulled out, and ran over to the chimney. It was on the south side of the building, and she did her best to climb up it while remaining hidden. Once on the top, she looked around and the men had indeed moved around to the northern side. Without hesitation, Kirsten planted her left foot, pushed off the chimney, and outstretched her arms.

She dropped like a stone. The first ten feet, she dropped. The next ten, she felt a slight buoyancy, and by the time she was thirty feet down, the kite jacket had caught. She glided out around ten feet above the ground, covering a distance she couldn't have hoped to have got to. She arrived at the fence on the south side, well clear of the building.

Had they even seen her? Did they even know what she'd done? Kirsten didn't care, but hurdled the fence and ran off into the trees. She completed the first hundred yards before she felt the material from the kite jacket catching on branches. She reached behind her shoulders, diving into her pack and pulling out a knife. Quickly, she cut away the material, letting it fall to the ground. There was no time to be sentimental about something that had saved her life.

Kirsten lifted her knees and ran through the trees. Behind her, she could hear the dogs. She had noticed none previously. Where had they come from? She'd have to head for a river. Maybe she could break across open water to knock them off the scent. As she ran hard to the south, the dogs faded into the background.

It took Kirsten about twenty minutes to run the remaining mile or so to her car. When she arrived, she crouched in the shadows, watching it, making sure no one else was watching it. Then she ran out and quickly looked underneath it.

The car seemed untampered, but then again, there were so many cars out here. People had parked up here, there, wherever; walkers and hikers. It could have been anyone's. That was why she'd left it so far away.

Taking off her backpack, she threw it into the car, started it up, and drove. Kirsten had come away with something. She'd come away with a coded plan, although whether anyone could break its code would be another matter. She'd come away with pictures of the inner sanctum of Lord Hugh. Maybe there'd be more in there that she'd be able to uncover. Most importantly, she'd come away with her life.

Kirsten turned and headed back towards Inverness, driving

by the west side of Loch Ness. When she reached the city, she headed back out into the countryside and drove to her shack. There in the underground bunker, secured, she stripped off and washed herself down with a packet of baby wipes.

Life was undignified when you had to resort to these measures, but the safe house was what it was, safe. She looked at the cans within it and made herself some soup before catching a few hours' sleep. All the while her mind was churning; what to do next? She'd need to speak to Justin, see if they got any more out of Danny Kyle.

The main thing that was bothering Kirsten, though, was what was Craig doing in all this. More importantly, how was she going to get him out of it? She wanted to turn him around. She wanted to make him whole again, not physically, obviously. He'd have to learn to use prosthetics. Maybe have to learn to stand on his own feet, so to speak, but she wanted to let him know she wasn't against him. He was the man she loved. He was the man she'd given everything up for before Zante. If he could turn to this, though—

There was a demon in her head. It had to be a demon because of what it spoke. It told her that Craig was always like this, that Craig was just using her when he disappeared off with her. She was just a prize, a trophy, an impressive figure, and a great mind, something to play with. When things had gone wrong, he'd thrown her away. The demon came and haunted her constantly. As much as she pushed that thought away, it came right back to her.

What did she really have though, after all this effort? She was no nearer Craig, and the Service was becoming less and less reliable for her. Kirsten needed to know where she stood, where everybody stood. She needed to get a better plan out of this and wanted to save Craig. She'd call a meeting between the few people she could trust. Justin, she could trust him. He'd always been trustworthy. Anna Hunt, she could probably trust her to do the decent thing. She could trust her integrity in trying to achieve a sensible outcome, and then Godfrey; the only thing about him she could trust was his self-interest.

Chapter 12

Godfrey was not a man who got rattled easily. In all his years, he had kept a cool head, and he would not let that go now. He had often admired other networks of spies, other countries, at what they did, none more so than the Israelis. If something was happening within his organisation, there was a strong possibility the Israelis knew about it.

They wouldn't be orchestrating it or even assisting from the side. A strong UK spy network wasn't against the Israelis. After all, they had been allies, many times, and Israel needed all the allies they could get.

The man he was going to meet, he had known for many years. He wasn't quite at the top of the Israeli Service, but he wasn't far from it. Highly respected, he was more of an advisor these days than an operator, but an advisor with many years. He still had people around the globe feeding him information, people deeply buried into organisations. All the rumours, all the chats, still came to him.

To meet with someone like this, especially at such short notice, you had to head somewhere private, somewhere easy for him to get to, but somewhere you trusted.

In some ways, Dingwall was nowhere. A town just outside Inverness with a rival football club. In the greater schemes of the world, it was nowhere, but it was home to a small flat above the laundry shop. A flat owned by Godfrey, a flat that had held in its time many meetings. Most of them the Service didn't know about. He was no traitor, but Godfrey knew when those meetings had to be truly secret. None of them had been noted.

None of the actions taken from them, or the results of information fed through, had been recorded. It was information that could have got him, or other people, killed. His contacts trusted him. Godfrey had gone to Cambridge with this Israeli contact. In fact, they'd been good friends, but now, they were old friends. Because they worked in different areas, they had a professional wariness, but still a good-natured relationship. If Godfrey was under this much threat, Peter would tell him.

The driver dropped Godfrey just outside Inverness, and he walked twenty minutes to get onto a bus. That bus took him to Dingwall, and once there, Godfrey got off at a stop, approximately a mile and a half away from where he wanted to be. The town wasn't particularly busy. The day was overcast.

As Godfrey made his way through the car park of a retail outlet and down an alleyway towards the door for his flat, the laundrette underneath was open. The world seemed to progress normally.

As Godfrey took out the key to open the door, he heard footsteps. He looked behind him, and there was a man, at least a foot taller than him, and possibly a foot wider. A brute, there to intimidate, maybe there to capture. He looked the other way and, coming from the main street through an alleyway, was a younger woman. She walked in boots with jeans, a chequered shirt, looking like a hiking tourist. The pair walked quickly towards Godfrey.

He continued to open the door and let the key remain in the lock as it swung open. Then, he calmly turned, looking both ways, and decided that the woman probably posed a greater threat. He reached slowly inside his jacket, looking for his gun. It was there, and as he withdrew it, and turned to fire, he found the trigger finger seized, unable to move.

Most men at this point would've panicked, but Godfrey returned the gun to its holster. He would need to check that later. Instead, he allowed a small knife to descend from his sleeve and come into his left hand. He turned towards the big man. He was now only five feet away. With his left hand however, Godfrey let the knife fly behind him. The big man reached for him.

Godfrey stepped to one side. He could hear gurgling behind him. That would be the knife in her throat. With another knife slipping out into his right hand, he cut along the lower legs of the man, causing him to cry out and drop to the ground. He then bent down and punctured the man's neck.

It was more of a bloody mess than he wanted to make. Godfrey grabbed the man's feet and dragged him inside. As he got him just clear of the door, he hurried back outside and dragged the woman inside, too. Then he shut the door. He bolted it top, bottom, and middle. Walking upstairs into the flat, he picked up the phone.

Godfrey dialled a number, and the man on the other end read out a series of numbers. Godfrey read out a series of numbers back. Codes having been exchanged, he asked for assistance.

'Lockdown, this is my location,' said Godfrey, aware he was

giving up one of his best safe houses. He wouldn't have to tell his Israeli contact not to come. There was always going to be a bit of commotion, and his friend would see people who shouldn't really be there—Godfrey's cleanup crew, getting rid of the bodies he has disposed of.

'Do you require assistance, sir?' asked the voice at the end of the line.

'I need to clean up. I also need Brenda. Tell her to bring the bike.'

He put the phone down and walked over to the kitchen. It was nothing spectacular. A small two-ring burner, kettle on the side, microwave in the corner. He didn't cook spectacular meals here. It was a functional place, and so he put the kettle on. He looked up at the jars in the cupboard, pulled out a tea bag, and dropped it into a cup. It was crude, but frankly, at the moment, he needed it.

Having allowed the tea bag to steep for several minutes, Godfrey removed it and took his black tea out to the stairs that led up to the flat. The door at the bottom was still locked. He stared at the bodies there. What a waste of two good operatives, he thought. Well, they weren't that good.

He wondered where they'd come from, but inside, he knew they were part of the Service. The technique, the way they used a pincer movement. They'd kept their distance, kept away, so he hadn't seen them coming, but how had they known he'd be here? Because that's what they had done.

They hadn't been tailing him, not in the car. Not since he got off onto the bus. They must have known where he was going. They would have to have been waiting. Godfrey's cup shook as he thought about this. That was what truly frightened him. People were operating inside the Service without Godfrey knowing.

Godfrey was the Service. Godfrey was the arms, the legs, the eyes, the ears, everything. He was the god of the Service. If something happened in it, he knew about it. He gave the go or the nay, and someone was taking that off him.

He finished his tea and went back inside to sit on the sofa. When he heard a knock downstairs, there were two sharp knocks. Then long pauses between three other knocks and then a four-time quick knock followed. It was Brenda, but still he went down with a weapon in hand to open the door.

Brenda stepped inside, looked down at the bodies, and then give Godfrey a wide smile.

'Good to see that you're safe, sir,' she said. Brenda was six feet two and had shoulders you could put a house on either side of. She was quick. She was lithe. Some man might have thought she was good-looking as well, but Godfrey hadn't been interested in that. She was an excellent personal bodyguard, and she was fiercely loyal to him. She always had been.

'Where's the bike?'

'Just outside. Do you wish to go now?'

'Somebody knew I was here, Brenda, somebody knew where I was coming. I need to go now.'

Together, they walked down the stairs, stepped over the bodies, opened the door, and closed it behind them. Godfrey put on a helmet and sat behind Brenda after she had mounted the bike.

He hated motorbikes. You go by car. Car was the best, but Brenda getting here was what he really needed. He didn't need a Service car. She would've seen one of his secret abodes. One she'd never seen, but at least he could trust her. She'd keep his secret. Even if she'd worked out that he had places running that the Service didn't know about, she knew all the Service ones. That was her job. She would take him to one of them whenever they got in trouble.

Brenda took the bike along the main road out of Dingwall and then looked to head back towards Inverness. Before she could reach the city, she turned off towards Muir of Ord, travelling down backcountry roads. She took a left down what was only a farmer's track. The bike wasn't built for long-distance road travel; it was built to get out of anywhere in a hurry, and it managed the track without a sign of weakness.

Godfrey wasn't sure where Brenda was going. However, she may have been taking him to a car. He couldn't really communicate at the moment. His arms were around her waist, and she drove along in front, almost impassively. Only the arms were moving as she turned a corner. The bike tore down the track, stones flying here and there. Godfrey thought about how someone had known. How had they?

A pain ripped through his thigh. He looked down to see a knife in it. A knife that Brenda had delivered. She was leaning back now; she drove the elbow of her other arm into his stomach. Godfrey pitched backward and fell off the bike.

He landed hard on his shoulder, crying out in pain, but it was stifled by the helmet he was wearing. His head hit hard as well, but the helmet had done its job. Up ahead, the bike slowed, turned, and was coming back towards him. Inside, there was a desperation. *Brenda*, he thought, *not Brenda. She looked after me. Brenda was mine*. He had thought Brenda more loyal than even Anna Hunt. Brenda would obey. She would do the dirty work. Brenda would get him out of there. Yet, Brenda had just stabbed him and she was coming back for more.

The years of experience, training, and the relentless drive

for perfection meant that Godfrey, while shocked, went into automatic pilot. He waited there, simulating an injury that was much worse than what he'd sustained. Godfrey was truly hurting; he was truly sore, but he drove those from his mind and instead, watched Brenda approach.

There was a vulnerable point. When you got off the bike, there was a vulnerable point as long as she didn't drive over him. But Brenda stopped short as she swung her leg off the bike. She stepped backward away from it, reaching in with her hand to her jacket, probably finding a gun.

It was at that point Godfrey knew he had her. There was no emotion. As the knife slipped into his right hand from up his sleeve, it departed his right hand, and in a mere second, it was buried in the Brenda's throat. Her helmet had exposed her throat for the merest of seconds.

She toppled backwards, trying to clutch at her throat, but the blade had sunk deep. She gurgled, blood spurted out, and Godfrey continued to lie on the ground for a moment. Knowing she was gone, he felt a heavy heart.

Who is doing this? Who is coming after me? How had they got to Brenda? She didn't need money. Brenda had money. She joined the Service to do duty by her country.

How do you turn someone like this? Godfrey picked himself up. His trousers were ripped on one side. His leg was in severe pain where the knife had gone through. He took his jacket off and then ripped an arm, tying it tight over his thigh. The wound had opened badly, but the tourniquet he would make would soon stop it. He walked over to the bike, almost swearing at it, but he picked it up and got the bike started.

He jumped on, looking over at the body of Brenda. *What a waste*, he thought, *a total waste*. He said this to himself because his hands were shaking. They were coming for him, and he couldn't see where they were coming from. He couldn't see how they were doing it. Who could he trust now? Who was actually trustworthy?

The irony wasn't lost on Godfrey as he rode the bike away. He had spread lies and counter-lies. He had assessed who he could tell what to. Godfrey had played people off against each other and now he was talking about trust to work out who had tried to kill him. He was pondering his people, especially with the position he was in. He hoped he wasn't wrong about many of them.

Chapter 13

Loch Ness was much deeper than it was wide, but it was also home to boats that would traverse the loch. Making way down the Caledonian Canal, they climbed up the locks at Fort Augustus before continuing along towards Fort William. Kirsten reckoned there was enough other traffic they wouldn't look out of place. She had hired this vessel for the day from a cruise company, but didn't tell them her purposes in doing so. She had paid handsomely and said she just needed some time out. However, as she passed under her first bridge on the way out of Inverness, someone dropped onto the boat.

Kirsten was sitting with the ship's wheel in front of her, steering as it putted along. There wasn't a substantial amount of speed, and it'd be a while before she picked up her next two passengers. The rear doors of this holiday cruiser opened, and a man entered in jeans and a T-shirt. Kirsten wasn't sure she'd ever seen him like that. He also wore a flat cap that really didn't suit him.

'I don't think anyone followed you,' said Justin Chivers.

'How far did you trace me?'

'Since you picked the boat up. Are they coming?'

'Yes,' said Kirsten. 'Go down below. There's a stove and a kettle. Make me something. Coffee, tea, whatever they've got.' Justin disappeared down below and came back up five minutes later, placing a cup of coffee in front of Kirsten.

'Are you sure about this?' asked Justin.

'Pulling us all together? Why?'

'Godfrey won't like it. I don't know if he's trusting anyone at the moment. You heard he was attacked.'

'I think we've all been attacked. There's a lot of it going around.'

'No, but Godfrey was attacked by Brenda. Brenda's his personal bodyguard. Brenda's the one who sorts people out if it's required. You've never met Brenda. Some in the Service have, and there are others outside of the Service who did. They have gone to meet their maker as well.'

Justin looked over, raising his eyebrows. 'Brenda was a surprise to Godfrey. You don't do this game without being betrayed on occasions, but you get people you trust. Truly trust.'

'And who do you truly trust?' asked Kirsten.

'You, for a start. I'm here. You could dispose of me anytime you wanted.'

'But why?' asked Kirsten. 'I'm being paid to do a job. I'm not part of the Service.'

'You're always part of the Service,' said Justin. 'They own you from the moment you sign up. Oh, you can walk away, but you'll never leave.'

'You sound like a bad '70s song,' Kirsten replied. 'Anyway, about half an hour, we'll pick up the next one and then the one after that, about an hour later. So, there's going to be plenty of time for pleasant conversations. Let's hope your jokes get better.'

'I'm not joking. You never leave. It always believes that it owns you. They always think they own you. Yes, they pay money out but . . .'

'Is that why you don't go? You've probably seen enough, haven't you?'

'More than you could know,' said Justin, 'but this, this is crazy. Somebody has dismantled the Service. Somebody has turned so many people. It's incredible. I don't understand it.'

'No, I don't either.'

The pair remained in silence, drinking their coffee until passing through another lock, at which point a woman appeared and ran on to their boat. She entered through the rear door while Justin was out assisting at the lock. Sitting down in the corner, she put her feet up on the long sofa-like bench. She didn't say a word until Justin was back inside.

'Do I get coffee too?'

'I'm on the wheel and I get paid to do what I do,' said Kirsten. 'I'm not making coffee.'

'I'll get the coffee,' said Justin, and slouched down below to the galley.

'Do you think it's wise bringing us?' asked Anna Hunt.

'Don't you start,' said Kirsten. 'Yes, it is wise. We need to be together. We need to sort out how to deal with this. Godfrey's not. Godfrey's—'

'Compromised. Chickens coming home to roost,' said Anna. Anna Hunt stood up and walked over to Kirsten. She stood behind her and placed a hand on her shoulders. She gently rubbed them. 'And how are you doing? You saw him. Is he still him? Is he?'

'You don't need to go through that,' said Kirsten. 'He is what he is now. We get on with it.'

'You can try to,' said Anna. 'I've been there before. You're not the only one that's been betrayed in this game, and by someone so close.'

Justin appeared from the galley with two cups and looked over. 'Getting very intimate,' he said, placing the cups down, 'or do you do back rubs for everyone?'

'With your reputation, there's no way I'm coming near you,' said Anna. Justin laughed. His reputation, the stud of the Service, the man who used women left, right, and centre, and yet in reality, a man who had never gone to bed with a woman in his life. He laughed. 'Before Godfrey gets here,' said Anna, taking a more serious tone, 'do you trust him?'

'I trust his money.'

'Why, Kirsten? Why do you trust his money?'

'You brought me in from the outside. Why? What's the point? If he's behind all this—if he's—'

'He can't be behind this,' said Justin. 'There's no purpose to it for him.'

'Godfrey's purposes are long and winding,' said Anna. 'It takes a long journey to get to the end of them, but for what it's worth, I don't think he's behind this one. He wouldn't have disposed of Brenda. He liked Brenda, truly liked Brenda. Godfrey doesn't have a like that for most people. He's never really had it for me.'

'How do you think he's doing it?' asked Kirsten. 'How do you think people are being turned? These were loyal people.'

'You think? What do you know about the Service? How loyal do you think people are? How many do you think have sought to leave and have been kept in play by Godfrey? Just how many people do you think Godfrey has things on? He has plenty on you.'

'No, he doesn't,' said Kirsten.

'Yes, he does. You're here. He understands you still have a desire for the action. You don't like sometimes where that takes you, but he still gets you back here. I haven't left either. Neither has Justin.'

'You haven't left because you want to do the decent thing. You believe in this country. Anna, you believe in—'

'Exactly, and he manipulates that. People can be turned when they realise that they're being used. This game, this spy game we play, is all about using people. It's all about taking what they can offer and aiming them. The hell with them and their lives.'

'It can't be true to that depth,' said Kirsten.

'Look at you. Look at what happened,' said Anna. 'Look at me. I'm a battered shell of a woman compared to what I used to be. I have taken many a beating, and many a time in this line of work, I have sacrificed things, things a woman shouldn't have to sacrifice.' She stared at Kirsten, and Kirsten knew what she meant.

'We have to work out how we're going to end it, as well,' said Justin. The boat fell silent and remained so until they berthed by a small jetty where a man in a suit stepped on board, an umbrella with him. The day was drizzly. He said nothing but sat in the corner as Kirsten took the boat out into the middle of Loch Ness and then allowed the boat to drift as she switched the engine off.

'I'll start,' said Godfrey suddenly. 'I have brought many people in. Truly, I have sought to find out who is behind this and yet no one knows.'

'You haven't been able to find out?' said Kirsten. 'You haven't been able to break anyone?'

'No one knows. I have broken so many people in this career of mine. Do not underestimate my talents, Miss Stewart. No one knows. So many of them.'

'Is there any link between them? Any?'

'No, there isn't. There is no link. They're all Service operatives. They're all turning. I'm desperate enough that I went to see an Israeli colleague. That's when they attacked me. They seem to know everything. They seem to be on to me. People second guess my moves. I got attacked, and I never saw them coming because they knew where I was going. They knew about my secret hideaway. It's a nothing place. I visited always in disguise and yet there they were. Brenda attacked me. This is beyond,' said Godfrey.

Kirsten was used to Godfrey being sharp; Godfrey being the one who could handle whatever was thrown at him, the one who told her and Anna things they didn't know. A smooth operator, a complete operator, and here he was babbling, leaving his dirty laundry out on the floor.

'Lord Hugh's estate has been compromised. It's gone. We've tried satellite imagery. I need to find where else they have hideouts. We're struggling to get any information from the photos you sent me through,' said Godfrey to Kirsten. 'We are—' He suddenly stopped, gripping his umbrella. 'We are compromised beyond all belief. There's no trust in the Service.'

'Trust?' said Kirsten. 'When did the thing ever operate on trust?'

'It's always operated on trust and honour. It has to. There has to be an underlying element of trust, a belief that says that we trust each other to do the best for the country. That trust has always stayed. That trust has always been intrinsic,' said

Godfrey.

'Well, you blew it for one,' said Justin, 'when you blew up that Russian woman. And then everyone saw what happened to Craig. We had to trust you to protect him, protect the best interest. People are quite happy to lay down their lives when—'

'What do you know, Chivers?' said Godfrey, suddenly. 'Tell me, what do you know about sacrifice? What do you know about—'

'Enough,' said Anna Hunt. 'Enough. We are the Service, the people who keep this country together. We have prevented terrors and disasters and we will continue to do so and we will not fight amongst ourselves just because things are falling apart. Calm, please.'

Anna walked to the end of the cabin, looking out to Loch Ness. 'My investigations are coming up with leads that are shut down so very quickly. There's no apparent agenda for what's going on. There's no reasoning behind it. People have left their official buildings. They're scared to work. Things are grinding to a halt. But why? Who would want to take our Service out?'

'Russians,' said Justin, 'want to bring down our network.'

'For what purpose? Are we the biggest threat to them? I don't think so. There are plenty of others and there's plenty of other Services that benefit from us, who would want to keep it afloat. I believe this is internal. This is not from others. I believe somebody wants to take down the house from inside.'

'Beliefs are all fine,' said Kirsten, 'but what do we do? How do we act against them because at the moment we can get no traction?'

'We still have a link,' said Justin. 'Mark Lamb. Mark Lamb provided the bombs to these people.'

'There's also Craig,' said Kirsten. 'Craig is a link. He was there. He was there with Lord Hugh.'

'And not been seen again,' said Godfrey.

'And what is he doing?' asked Justin. 'Why did they bring in a man in a wheelchair? What has he got to offer? The secrets with half the Service turned? Who cares about them? What is he able to do? Why is he at the forefront? Is he uniting them? Is his story compelling enough? Has he got enough to actually run this?'

'We've got a hit,' said Kirsten. 'He's got enough on me and the rest of you.'

'Then we need to go after Craig. We need to see what he's up to,' said Anna.

'Yes, we do, but Kirsten, foremost, you need to go after Mark Lamb. He's provided the weaponry, but he has no angst against the Service. He's a mercenary who builds bombs. Go after him, Kirsten,' said Godfrey. 'Go after him and get me a link through to these people.'

'But what about Craig? I can get to Craig,' said Kirsten.

'No,' said Godfrey. 'Anna will go after Craig. You're too close to Craig.'

'But he might let me speak to him.'

'No,' said Anna. 'Trust me. When they turn like this, when this happens, you'll use your guilt to bring them in. You'll use your guilt to say that you can save them. They'll have no such guilt. You do that and Craig will kill you. I will go after Craig.'

'If there's a chance, Anna.'

'There won't be,' she said.

'Good. That's decided,' said Godfrey. 'And Chivers, get working on that documentation Kirsten got us. We need a breakthrough from that. We have the Service on its knees and we have nothing. It's time to fight, ladies and gentlemen. It's time to pick ourselves up. I'm losing too many good people, and I don't know why.'

Chapter 14

'How are we going to get a hold of Mark Lamb?' asked Justin. He was sitting across from Kirsten in her Inverness flat, sipping on a cup of black coffee she'd served him. He noticed she didn't sit down, but would pace back and forward, walking here and there with her cup in her hand.

'We need to get in under the radar. We need to come in as a faction that can work for him. Obviously, they're aiming at the establishment, or maybe we can come as being anti-establishment.'

'Obvious, pretending to come in after the Service ourselves.'

'Not the Service,' said Kirsten. 'We can't come in going after the Service. It fits the bill too nicely. No, we'll be the people here going after local governance and things like that. A line up beside what they're doing. After all, they're going to need bodies to help with the Service.'

'How do you get their attention, then?' asked Justin.

'We'll start off with a little low-level vandalism. Break a few windows here and there. Maybe even handcuff the odd policeman.'

'It needs to be quick, though.'

'It does. Three nights on the bounce. That's what it'll take,' said Kirsten. 'Three nights on the bounce to get a name for ourselves. We'll get in the paper. As soon as we're in the paper, we can start pitching to some other people that we want something higher. Maybe looking at a bomb or something. It's not the best plan in the world, is it?' said Kirsten.

'I agree. Normally, it should be much more drawn out. Several months. We haven't got several months. The way Godfrey's looking and talking, we may not have a Service in several months. It's a risk we're going to have to take. What are you proposing, then?'

'Well,' said Kirsten. 'I think the first one has to be quite simple. Big, but quite simple.'

The next morning, Justin was back in her flat with a bunch of headlines from the online papers.

'They won't reach the physical copies yet. They'll be in later, but I think you got noticed.'

Kirsten grabbed the sheets of paper Justin was holding out. She was looking at the main shops within Inverness. Also, the bridge over the Eastgate Centre. The side walls towards the main square where the train station exited. Everywhere was graffitied. Simple, but effective. It had taken a bit of time and she got chased in the early hours of the morning. But she had moved from one to the other, continuing her artistic tirade.

'You certainly caused a flutter,' he said. 'I think part one went successfully.'

'I think it did. Are they going to have any more officers out tonight, do you know?'

'Given the press coverage you're getting, I would say so. You were on the back end of the morning news as well.'

'That's good,' said Kirsten. 'That's good because tonight, we

111

step it up a bit.'

The following morning, Justin returned. More printouts from the internet.

'How many police cars did you actually steal?'

'Six,' said Kirsten. 'I didn't damage them too badly. They should be back in service by tonight.'

'Stealing them and putting them near every public urinal there was. Clever. Sending a statement without actually harming anyone. Brilliant. It's not enough, though. It's very low level. How are you going to show that you want to harm someone?'

'I do need to show that I want to harm someone, don't I? If the likes of Mark Lamb are going to believe I want a bomb, I'm going to have to show that I'm prepared to take life. I'm going to need your help tonight with this one,' she said.

'Always. What's the plan?'

'Kidnap a police officer. Set him up in a video link as if I'm going to despatch him. You're going to phone it in before I can do it and I'll leg it away.'

'Nice,' said Justin.

That evening, the pair executed their plan and were back in the flat at approximately five in the morning.

'It went well,' said Justin.

Kirsten nodded. However, she didn't look happy.

'You had to do it. You didn't harm anyone.'

'I held a knife to his throat. I scared the living hell out of him. Of course, I hurt him. I've given him a mental scar that he'll never get over. I can't exactly walk around and apologise and say, oh, by the way, time's a healer, can I?'

'I suppose not. Hopefully, that should be the last. You've carried out three unique acts now. Three different nights ramping it up. Hopefully, Mark Lamb will think there's a player in town. A player that wants to get better at what she does. When are you going to make the contact?'

'We'll reach out tonight. Low level. Scale it up. Go through them until we can go up higher.'

'Do you need me with you on that?'

'Probably best. It'll look like we're more than just one person. Look like a bigger team. There'll be another night of work, but after that, hopefully, we'll be where we need to be.'

Kirsten and Justin Chivers spent the evening working through various low-level arms dealer contacts. They felt like they got bounced from here to there. They explained that the last three nights of terror were looking to crescendo by the weekend. Yet, they were running short of a suitable device to cause an explosion on the unsuspecting town of Inverness.

It took a couple of dealers before the name of Mark Lamb was mentioned, and several hours before a meeting was going to be arranged. They told Kirsten it would cost several thousand pounds, which she agreed to. It would also be a week. Kirsten insisted on quicker. Eventually, a meeting was set for two days' time. There was a gala ball for charity happening in a hotel on the edge of Inverness. She was advised to attend, a ticket would be sent to her, and to look for a Frederick Jones.

On the evening in question, Justin arrived at Kirsten's flat to find the door opened by a woman in a dress.

'Blimey,' he said. 'It's rare we see you like that. You're always happier in your jeans.'

'I can dress too,' she said. 'What I don't like is the footwear. How do us women move about in these things?'

Justin laughed. 'One of the good things about being a man. You don't have to have those ridiculous things on, but you look good. That's coming from a man who doesn't want to look either.'

'If you think I'm trusting your opinion about this, you've got to be joking.'

She walked across her room in a black dress that stopped around mid-thigh. There were two narrow shoulder straps, and most of the back was missing. In a lot of ways, she hated how she looked. This wasn't Kirsten—feeling like a piece of meat.

She never quite understood the women who dressed up in this sort of finery as if they were the ones in charge. Kirsten always felt that she was on parade, made to look how someone else wanted her to look. At this point in time, that was fine. After all, this was her job, and she was getting paid. She was only playing a role, but it was a role she would never have in real life. Still, she would try to capture Mark Lamb tonight using the good old female techniques of attraction, lust, and the promise of something more.

Justin drove Kirsten to the front door of the hotel before dropping her off and then sat in the car, parked outside. Justin didn't like the car park. There were some walls around it, a few alleys off it, and unlike hotels with plenty of countryside around them, there was a housing estate. It was never an easy escape route. He couldn't see the field of play. There were too many places to hide, too many places for people to take a pop shot.

Kirsten strode into the gala ball across the hotel lobby with its hanging golden lights. She met a woman in a long red dress who checked her ticket. Kirsten was under the name of Francine Claire and checked the table arrangements to see Kirsten's table and seating position. Frederick Jones was also at her table.

Kirsten walked to the bar, ordered a glass of wine, and then walked to the table. She wasn't the tallest, most elegant woman in the room. That prize would be taken by others. She was one of the smallest women there, but Kirsten was trim, and she'd happily be in this company without feeling inferior. It was just a pity you couldn't get any of them into a ring. If your body was only good for looking at, you weren't anything in Kirsten's book; you had to be able to fight. That's how she was brought up, and that was how she gauged how her body looked.

Frederick Jones sat in a black tuxedo, staring up at her as she arrived at the table. She walked over, holding out her hand, and he stood up, took it, and kissed it.

'Francine Claire,' she said. 'And you are?'

'Frederick Jones, I believe our companies have made contact,' he said. 'Please, won't you sit with me for a while?'

Kirsten sat down, and Frederick pointed out various parts of the gala. Most of his chat was banal, until he turned around to her and said, 'I hear you're wishing to make an impact on the market.'

'Indeed,' she said. 'I've heard good things about your methods for opening markets up wide; very sudden, quick, extremely effective. One of the best operators in the game. I may be just getting into the game, but I'm looking to make a big impact.'

She watched his hand slide across onto her thigh and he rubbed back and forward across it.

'You certainly look in shape, and from what I've seen of your previous work, you are indeed beginning to make a mark, but we all need backers. Have you got the backing? Have you got the finances to hit the market at this speed? Maybe it would be better for you to slow down a little, approach it bit by bit, start off smaller and build up and scale. I'm not saying there isn't a future for you. I think there is a wonderful future. Maybe we can collaborate.'

He moved his hand higher up her thigh, and Kirsten put a hand down onto his. 'I tend to be careful about mixing business and pleasure unless I know that the business is concluded.'

'Maybe we should explore exactly what it is you want to do.'

'Maybe,' she said. 'And then maybe afterwards we could celebrate, but we'll need somewhere better than this to explore.'

'I have a room upstairs. We could go up there and talk, settle things, and then maybe enjoy the rest of the evening.'

'That sounds terrific,' said Kirsten, smiling. 'Sometimes you worry if you can get ahead in this game, but to know there's people out there willing to build up trust together.'

'I think we'll be doing a lot of trust-building once the business is concluded tonight.'

Kirsten leaned over, placing her hand on his thigh. 'Plenty of trust building,' she said. 'Shall we discuss things?'

She stood up and found him by her side quickly. He led her over to the lift in the lobby, pressing for floor five once inside. She felt his hand on her bare back, moving up and down before settling on her backside.

He's hooked, she thought. *He's definitely hooked.*

The man was older than she expected. Lamb had grey hair on either side of a staunch face, which warmed up when he looked at her. He was currently smiling, thinking he had her tonight. He'd laid his trap, and he'd have more than business. They walked towards his room, the door of which he opened and let her inside. It wasn't quite a full suite, but there was a table beside a large bed, and he poured a drink from the minibar.

'This okay? I like it, and I like it neat.'

'Of course,' said Kirsten. She took it from him and downed it.

'You're quite a spunky girl, aren't you?' he said. Lamb threw his back.

'Sit on the bed,' she said. 'I'll pour the next one.'

She stayed with her back to him and heard him sit down on the bed. With a sleight of hand from a fold in her dress, she took out a tiny phial, cracking the lid of it almost soundlessly. A few drops went into his tumbler. Kirsten filled the rest up with vodka and then filled her own glass.

She'd have him soon. He'd be out for the count. After a couple of sips, she turned, holding both tumblers, and walked over to him. But as she did so, her left leg buckled slightly.

'Damn stilettos,' she said. 'I'm much more of a country girl.'

'I think you're much more of a martial arts girl,' said the man, smiling. Quick to get your notoriety. Quick to be looking for a bomb. Way too quick, in fact.

Kirsten went to run forward, but her left knee buckled again. Her hand let the tumbler slip out of it, and she fell, her head hitting the soft mattress of the bed before she fell backwards onto the ground. Everything was going woozy, the world slipping away from her, but she felt him bind her arms behind her back. Her legs were also being tied together, and then she felt nothing at all.

Chapter 15

J ustin Chivers sat in the car feeling a little anxious. He'd seen Kirsten disappear through the windows of the hotel, out towards the lobby, and then presumably upstairs. That was fine because it was all part of the plan, but she was going to drug him, and Mark Lamb was going to be taken away by the pair of them. Kirsten still hadn't come down to ask for his help.

It was too long because the last thing she would've done on getting him alone was let it drag out. It would've been quick, and then she would've signalled, getting Justin in to help her remove Mark Lamb from the building. Justin was also edgy because he needed to pee. Well, she wouldn't miss him for ten seconds.

He stepped out of the car and quickly disappeared into the shadows of one of the side alleys. After passing a quick ablution, he stepped back into the car park, emerging from the alley and doing what was a normal routine scan across the car park. As he did, there was no time to be surprised. There was no time to be shocked.

Across the car park, by another alley, was a man with a rocket launcher. Before he fired, Justin was already turning. By the time the rocket was racing towards his car, Justin was diving into the alleyway. When the explosion went up, Justin was in the other alleyway and was fortunate enough to be protected by the wall around a garden.

The dive had taken Justin off his feet, and he was lying on the ground when the full force of the explosion blew past him. He may have been hit by the odd piece of rubble. He wasn't sure, and he wasn't waiting around to find out. Instead, Justin was up on his feet as quick as he could, running as hard as he could.

His ears were ringing. He couldn't hear his feet thumping properly on the alleyway, and that caused him to stumble and wobble as he ran. The alleyway broke out into the street of a residential area, and Justin continued to run along it. Kirsten would be in trouble, though, and Justin ran up the main street to come round and back to the entrance of the hotel.

As he reached it, he could hear sirens in the night, the alarm bell of the hotel ringing because somebody had clearly set the fire alarm off as well. As he stood a short distance away, Justin stepped into the garden of a house, slipped behind a tree, and breathed deeply.

He had charged away. Then he charged back. Everything so far had been done on the hoof and done quickly. Now he stopped.

He would take thirty seconds to think, thirty seconds to suck in the air, to make a plan, and then go at it again. Justin needed to get in. He needed to see what was up with Kirsten. What was the best way to do that?

Hotel staff, he thought. *Hotel staff would still run around clearing the hotel*. It was time to get himself a uniform. Justin exited from behind the tree and ran towards the hotel again, but deviated towards the rear. There was an enormous wall there, but doors were opening and people were piling out onto the street.

These doors would not have been opened when the hotel was in normal use. With the panic that was happening, people were fleeing in whatever way they could.

Justin fought against the flow. He fought his way into the rear car park of the hotel. As he entered what he thought was the kitchen at the rear of the hotel, a porter came out. Justin stuck his hand out, grabbed the man by his throat, and pushed him back inside, driving him into an open cold store.

The kitchen was clearing. Most people had left and the bulk of them wouldn't be coming out through the kitchens. Only the staff would go this way.

Justin told the man to strip off his outer layers and changed into the outfit provided. He then yelled at the man to run out of the building, smacking his backside and the man tore off. Justin adjusted his clothing and left the kitchen.

Soon he was inside the hotel lobby with people screaming at him, hotel guests still running down from rooms up above. *Where had Kirsten gone?* he thought. He ran over to reception where he yelled, 'Did they have the lists of guests?' He was told they did, and he told them to get out. He would follow them quickly.

As soon as they turned, he looked at the check in computer screen in front of him. Justin understood computers. He understood systems, and it only took him a few moments to type in names. Frederick Jones. He must have had a room.

Floor five, room 514. He went to run for the lift, but of course, they could be shut down at any time. He bypassed the lifts and went to the emergency stairs.

'Where are you going?' shouted someone.

'We've got a guest up top. They need evacuation. I'm taking the stairs to get them down.'

'You'll need two of us.'

'It's all right. Someone's meeting me there. Get out, get out,' said Justin.

He tore off, leaving the man who had spoken to him. *Do everything quickly?* he thought. *Do it fast and do it like you mean it, and everyone will think you'll know what you're doing.' It doesn't matter how hard you train. When it's the real thing, people panic and somebody had blown up a car. And then they set off the alarms in the hotel.*

But they've been clever, he thought. *Caught her on her own potentially, and then taken me out. They've got her on the move.*

He hoped he wouldn't be too late. Justin reached the fifth floor, stepped out into the corridor, and looked along for a sign to say where the room numbers were. 506 to 520, down to the right. He turned and looked down. Someone was coming out of a room in a hurry.

Justin turned and walked down, but the other person raced off. Could have been anyone, though. After all, the hotel was being evacuated. There had been an explosion outside.

Justin walked quickly down to the room that the man had come out of. It was 514. He pushed open the door, looked inside. Nothing. Nobody in here. Then he saw the tumblers on the floor. *Had there been a struggle?* He looked down around him. *Were there any signs?*

And then he saw it, so, so small. It was one of the little dosing phials they would use when wanting to drop poison or some sort of sedative into someone's drink. You could sew it inside clothing, and it was so easy to miss.

It was on the floor, and the top of it was cracked. Kirsten had taken one. She'd been here; now she was gone. Instantly, Justin turned on his heel and started tearing down the hallway in the direction the man had left. As he reached the end of the corridor, he saw the emergency stairs. Justin turned and started sprinting down them.

After he completed four of the five flights of stairs, he saw the man in front of him about two flights down. He pursued him out of the building and watched as he got into a car. Justin watched the car drive off and realised he was on his own.

He couldn't very well run after him. He could try the license plate. By the time he organised anyone to get after it, the man would be gone.

He followed the car out into the mesh of traffic that was trying to escape the hotel. Police cars were now coming from the other way, and Justin could walk along the street, keeping the car in sight. Eventually, it broke the cordon of police coming the other way and sped up. Justin would not keep up, but ahead of him, he saw a woman in furs getting into a car, a chauffeur on the other side.

'Just get me out of here, James. Get me out of here and get me home. It's been a disaster. It's been a—'

The woman stopped as Justin put a gun in her face. 'James, get out of the car and leave the keys in the car,' he said. 'Madam, step away over there and James will stand beside you.'

Justin kept the gun trained on the woman. As he spun around the car, a police car raced down the street, but Justin held the gun in close.

'Don't go for it or I will shoot,' he said. 'James, get this good woman home in a taxi somehow. Apologies for your car, but I need it.' With that, Justin stepped inside the car, turned the ignition on with the keys, and drove off.

One of the good things about holding up somebody rich is that their car is of a good quality. This was a BMW, and it certainly could move. It didn't take long for Justin to find the car he was tailing further along the street. He settled back in his seat, wondering if Kirsten was inside that car in front.

He drove out of Inverness, first a little down the A9 and then broke off at Carrbridge, heading out onto smaller roads. Justin realised at any moment they could arrive at the destination. If they did, it could be more than whoever was in the car to deal with.

Was Kirsten alive or was Kirsten dead? Was she even in the car? He couldn't very well attack everyone once they arrived. He was one man on his own and, yes, he was Justin Chivers. Justin knew how to deal with people but not really large numbers, especially if any of them were experienced.

Justin closed up on the car and then, when he found a straight piece of road, he indicated, pulled past, and drove out of sight. As soon as he was clear, he stopped the car, put the hazard lights on, but left the car sitting across the road so it would be difficult to get past. He stepped out and started smacking the bonnet of the car.

The car he had been tailing came around the bend and halted. One man got out. 'What are you doing?' he asked.

'Fuel. Out of bloody fuel,' said Justin. 'Can you believe that? Can I get a siphon, or can you drop me down the road?'

'No,' said the man.

'Well, I'm stuck here. Come on. This time of night, the least you can do is get me down to a petrol station and back.'

'Move the car,' said the man. 'You need to move the car. We need to get past.'

'All I want is a petrol station,' said Justin. 'Can you imagine being out here? The wife will go spare. I'm meant to pick her up.'

'Where's your keys? I'll move the damn car,' said the man.

The driver of the other car now was getting out, something Justin had hoped for. While he was inside and behind the wheel, he could always tear away, and it'd be difficult for Justin to get at him; but not here. Not now.

'We don't want any trouble,' said the driver, 'but you need to move that car now. If you know what's good for you, you'll move it. You'll not argue; you'll just get on with it.'

'How am I meant to move it when it's run out of fuel?' asked Justin.

'We'll move it for you,' said the man. He stepped past Justin, opened the passenger door, and reached inside for the handbrake. The passenger of the other car came up as well. As he got closer, Justin grabbed him, pulling him in, and drove a knee up into his mid-rift. He then hit him on the back of the neck with a chop.

The other man heard the grunt and turned, pulling a gun out from his jacket. Justin was already at the door, closing it hard, and the man was caught between the door and the car.

Justin slammed the door against him four times before pulling him down and spotting the weapon still inside the jacket. He reached in, grabbed it, threw it away into the undergrowth, and then drew his own weapon.

'Both of you, on your knees. Do not move.'

Still groaning, the two men got on their knees, while Justin pointed the gun at them. He reached inside his jacket and took out the little glass phial that Kirsten had used previously back in Mark Lamb's room. He held the gun up to the head of one man, placed the phial inside the man's lips, and rubbed it back and forward. There wouldn't be much there, but the man would get a sensation of something.

'How well do you like Mark Lamb?' asked Justin. 'I've just poisoned you. You're going to tell me where he is. You're going to tell me his hideout, and you're going to tell me it quick because you need the antidote. If not, you'll be dead. I give you about two minutes.'

The man stared at Justin. The guy behind him said nothing. 'Just in case your mate thinks he's getting off scot-free, if you don't give the answer, he's getting the same treatment in a moment.'

The man looked at him, clearly afraid. Mark Lamb had some influence over these people, but Justin always thought your own life was worth something. Mark Lamb was a man who worked for money, so those that worked for him probably did too. He wasn't an idealist. Lamb wasn't running a cult. He was a bomber. He worked for money.

'One minute,' said Justin. 'Anytime now, you'll feel it. Of course, sometimes it works early, sometimes you get the dose wrong. It just—I don't know. It goes through the bloodstream. The science guys know all about it. They'll tell you how it works. You'll just feel it. Heard that's the worst of it, though.'

'This road. This road,' said the man suddenly, his breathing becoming erratic. Justin was stunned. He was producing effects even though the drug was nothing but a knockout drug, the dose of which wouldn't be enough to knock the man out.

'You'll need to keep going. It's a farmhouse further up. Cheshire farm. That's where he hangs out. Give me the antidote. Give me the antidote.'

'Cheshire Farm,' said Justin. 'People have lied to me before, and I only have one set of drugs.'

'It's bloody Cheshire Farm. Give me it. Give me it now. The antidote!'

'Thank you very much for your cooperation,' said Justin. 'There was nothing in that vial. Nothing at all.'

He took the butt of his gun and hit the man hard behind the head and then the other one as well, sending them both senseless to the floor of the road. He took out his phone, and dialled a number.

'Godfrey,' said Justin, 'I've got two men lying on the road out towards Carrbridge, coming out of Inverness. They've got Kirsten in Cheshire Farm farmhouse. I'm on my way to deal with it. I need you to come and collect two men on the road here, lest they get back and interrupt me. They're out cold. Don't know how long for. I'll tie them up with something. Push the car to one side. I don't know how I'll find her, though,' said Justin. 'Mark Lamb seemed to know we were coming. Unsure whether that was our bad execution or someone else.'

'Understood,' said Godfrey, and the call was closed.

Justin searched the other car, finding rope, and tied the two men up. The road was quiet enough, but it was five minutes after he tied them up and pushed the car off the road that the first of the cars pulled past. He got back into the BMW, however, and drove off. Godfrey had said nothing, and Justin wondered if he even trusted him. Did he think he'd killed Kirsten?

The trouble when everything went wrong with a spy organisation, Justin thought, *is that from thinking you know who to trust, you suddenly don't know who to trust at all. You see the intentions of everyone, or what you think are the worst intentions.* He trusted Kirsten, though, and Kirsten trusted him. It was time to see if she was still alive.

Chapter 16

There was darkness all around, but the floor kept bouncing. Every now and again, she felt pushed to one side and then back to the other. She was disorientated, wondering just where exactly she was. If only there'd been a chink of light. If only there'd been some way to—*Ow*, she thought, as her head smacked off something.

She'd rolled over onto her hands, which seemed to be bound behind her. Lying on them, she felt pain. She tried to push from her feet, but they were tied too. She couldn't yell because of the gag in her mouth, but her eyes were open. They just couldn't see anything.

She'd been stupid. Taking a drink without fully watching what he'd been doing. No, she hadn't been. She had fully watched him. He didn't have that great a sleight of hand; therefore, he'd known before. He'd known, and he played her all the way, letting her think it was her body that had enticed him up to that room. She laid a honey trap and he must've seen it coming. Now where was she?

She suddenly rolled again, a very short distance and her body hit off whatever wall was here. *No, it wasn't walls*, she thought, her hands feeling the surrounding surfaces. Slightly furry, but

128

firm. She was in the boot of a car. Kirsten realised that's why she kept rolling. That's why she felt the G-force when a car took a corner quickly. That's why there was the odd bump now and then. Was why she couldn't see.

No lights, nothing's to do until they arrived somewhere. Kirsten could try to work out the turns, the twists. She could lay there and listen for any sound that would give away where she was. Yet, there was nothing outside, nothing unique, and she didn't have a starting point, so the turns and twists were irrelevant.

She settled back, thinking about what to do. She was stuck, tied up. Could she free the bonds that held her? No, she couldn't. She had tried, but she couldn't. She would have to just sit and wait.

Inside, Kirsten felt sick. They'd captured her. She knew what they would do.

Eventually, the car stopped after going down what felt like a stony path. She heard car doors open and shut and then the boot opened. Her eyes looked up into the dim light. A pair of hands came down, pulled her out of the car, and another pair of hands wrapped themselves around her. She was taken through the door of a farmhouse, white.

In the distance, she thought she could hear the sea, but then she was taken to a room and unceremoniously thrown into the corner. The floor came up quickly. Kirsten cursed as it hit her. The men disappeared out of the room and she could hear voices outside before the two men came back inside with her.

They picked her up and dragged her into another room where someone produced a gun and put it in her face. Her hands were released before being handcuffed up above her head. She was then hooked to some sort of device that lifted her up, her feet leaving the ground so she was hanging by her arms. Kirsten felt the pain before she watched the man in front of her limber up.

He turned to his pal, putting down some money. Kirsten wondered what that was for. He turned and walked to her, looking up into her face.

'That's for whoever makes you shout out loud first. We'll break you. We'll break you.'

'No, no, no,' said Kirsten, the binds still in her mouth. The man reached up and pulled it down. 'What's that, dear?'

'You'll die along with him, but it'll be painful,' she said. 'I will break your back and once it's broken, I'll leave you, let you starve to death.'

Kirsten knew this was all talk, a way to instil fear back, but the man didn't seem that worried as he shoved the gag back up into her mouth. He stepped back and then drove a punch into her stomach. She swung on her arms, relieved that she could actually move backwards.

It would be worse if she tensed up against the punches. She'd taken many in her time, many beatings in the ring before, and here she couldn't fight back, her feet tied together, her arms up above her. Again, the man hit her, and again. When he went to hit her the next time, she swung her feet round, still bound, and caught him clean across the side of the face, sending him spiralling across the room. His friend laughed loudly.

'Bitch!' he yelled and turned and grabbed a metal pole on the side of the room.

'That's not playing the game,' his friend said to him. 'It's my go.'

He walked over and punched Kirsten in the stomach as well. She took punch after punch silently, and then she went to swing her legs, but he stopped; he moved himself out of reach as her legs went past. He then stepped in to punch her, but she'd seen it coming. Kirsten halted her swing and swung the legs back again, sending him spiralling into the room.

'Give me that pole,' the man said. 'Get one each,' his friend commented.

The two men picked up the poles before the door suddenly opened. An elegant blonde woman in a dress that revealed most of her right leg and the top of bare shoulders told both men to stop.

'That's enough fun, boys. We'll want her later. Her time will come. Don't worry.'

Kirsten stared at the woman. She walked up to Kirsten and, with a hand sporting painted red nails, pulled down the gag from her mouth.

'I'd apologise for what they're doing to you, but I told them to do it,' she said. The woman stepped back, clear of Kirsten's reach. 'My name is Emma. I'll not tell you my second name, but I will take everything away from you,' she said. 'Absolutely everything. I was warned about you, more dangerous than Anna Hunt, some seem to think, although hard to believe. More dangerous than Godfrey just sounds ridiculous, doesn't it? Godfrey is the dangerous one, after all.

'You dressed up well. I have to give that to you. You're not a lady, are you? You're a fighting dog with some nice fur. That's about it. Oh, I can see why you would entertain a man for a while, but ultimately, they'd want someone of class, someone who knows how to handle them, not some ragged bitch.'

Kirsten recognised her face. She'd been at the gala, but across from her at a different table, watching.

'I have nothing to have taken away from me,' said Kirsten.

'You're welcome to whatever.'

'Oh, you have plenty enough to have taken away from you. You haven't given up the ghost on things yet, have you?'

Kirsten didn't understand what the woman was saying. The door opened behind her and a man came in. Once through the door, the man stepped over to the shadows of the room, and Kirsten couldn't see him clearly. He was followed by another man, but this one was staggering.

'Is that her?' asked the first man.

'Yes,' said the second man, nodding.

'Get out.' The man who had identified Kirsten hobbled out of the room, and the door was closed. The man in the shadow continued watching her.

Emma walked up to Kirsten. 'You are no lady,' she said. 'Not at all.' She reached up, grabbing the straps of Kirsten's dress. 'No lady.'

The woman turned away briefly to the far side of the room before picking something up and returning. It was a knife and Kirsten tensed, wondering if the woman would stab her. Instead, she reached up to the straps at the top of her dress. She cut first one and then the other, and then she grabbed the dress, pulling it down hard until it came down off the end of Kirsten's feet.

Hanging in her underwear, Kirsten felt the cool of the farmhouse all around her now.

'Fighting dog, that's all you are, fighting dog with a bit of fur.'

She reached up, put the knife through the side of her underwear, cutting it loose, throwing first her bra to the floor, and then her underwear. This left Kirsten suspended naked.

'I think we'll let the men play with you before you're done.

Oh, they play properly with dogs. They won't treat you, well, like they do a lady.'

Kirsten steeled herself against the threats. If anybody came to touch her, to do anything to her, she'd fight even from this position. She'd kill a few. Inside, she was fearful, but she was being threatened in the worst way for a woman. What made it even more so was the fact it was a woman who was threatening, a woman who would tell them what to do.

'She'll need to be ready, though,' said a voice from the shadows. 'Maybe if she doesn't succeed, the men can have her. Until then, let her hang. We want it to be fair, don't we?' The man went to step out of the shadow but then stopped.

'Blindfold her,' he said. 'Then leave us.'

Kirsten didn't recognise the voice. It was gruff, but there was something about him. Emma got a pair of small steps, took a blindfold up to Kirsten, putting it over her eyes. Kirsten heard her step back down, then heard the door open and close.

'Just the two of us,' said the man. 'She's not lying, by the way. You'll be fighting for your honour, fighting for a chance, but the boys will have you. I'm not quite in agreement with her. I'm quite taken, in fact; strong and muscly, but you cut a figure.'

Kirsten felt a hand running up the side of her legs. Inadvertently, she twitched and began swinging from her bind above her.

'It's a pity what side you're on. I would fancy turning you, turning you over. We could have some good times as well. You're quite exceptional. I believe Anna Hunt was the one that recruited you. Anna's good, isn't she? Are you as devious as Anna? You're not as patient. Anna wouldn't have rushed through trying to get a hold of your bomber that quick. She'd have played it long, even if the fate of the Service was at hand.

'You don't have her skills in that sense, do you? Anna plays a very long game. She knows her enemies. She knows everyone around her. Older woman than you, beautiful in her own way. It's funny. Everyone thinks the men are hard, but I've been around enough of you to realise there's a coldness in a woman, especially in this game. Take Emma, for instance, very cold. Anna Hunt, one of the coldest, but you, you're different again. You're not that cold at times. Don't get killed tomorrow. At least don't get beat. I'd hate to see them clawing all over you.

'I may have stopped certain things tonight, but I won't be stopping things in the long run. I could try to offer you a pardon, a way out if you'd come and spend some time with me, but you'd only try to escape. That's the problem. You're too good, Kirsten. You want to be on the right side. It doesn't work when you're a spy. You can't be on the right side because sometimes your side is wrong. That's the way it plays out, isn't it? Still, such a pity.'

She felt the hand running down her back, across her bottom, down the back of her legs, and he seemed to kiss her hip. 'Such a pity,' came the words again.

She heard the door close, the cold of the air across her body. Her arms were feeling the strain of hanging there. *Would she get a way out?* For a moment, she thought about Craig, but this was not the time. This was the time to steel herself. This was the time to build up that hate, that anger, and channel it. He said she'd have to fight. He said the most horrible thing was awaiting her if she should lose. Lose, she would not. Kirsten would win or die trying.

Chapter 17

Justin Chivers was in a quandary. He didn't know who to trust. Currently, he was watching the farmhouse where Kirsten had been taken, or at least was thought to have been taken. He hadn't seen her from the outside or been in himself to find her. He had scanned the area. With the force that was at the farmhouse, he was unlikely to instigate a rescue, certainly not while she was inside.

He could easily go in, get trapped, and be lost without ever seeing her. He would also need some backup and weapons, but he didn't want to leave the farmhouse in case Kirsten emerged and was taken elsewhere. Although he hadn't identified that she was definitely in there, all intelligence said she was there. He could call Godfrey and ask for backup, but who would come? The Service was a mess. Who would trust him? Who did he trust? These things were racing through his head, while all he wanted to do was to get inside and find Kirsten.

Justin had always liked her. It wasn't many people in this game you found you could easily warm to and they never disappointed you. Anna Hunt was someone else he trusted, but Anna was different. Very professional. Never showed her cards until she really had to. She also worked with people that he struggled with.

Godfrey, for instance. Yes, he was the boss. You could follow orders, but Justin never trusted him. He wasn't sure Anna did, either. He thought through the other numbers he could call, people he'd worked with in the past. Could he say that any of them would've been on his trust list? It was Carrie-Anne and Dom who he'd worked with alongside Kirsten, but no, he wasn't sure about them now either.

They'd always been good colleagues to work with, but now they're outside the Service. Would you want to come into the middle of that? Would they just quit? Could they still get their hands on operational necessities? The longer you were out, the harder it was to come back in.

They had helped Kirsten before. Yes, they'd be willing, but they weren't the right people for this, and besides, he didn't know where in the world they were, and could they even get here quick enough? He thought through everything again and decided there was only one course of action, Anna Hunt. He stepped away a reasonable distance and dialled the number on his phone.

'Have you found him yet?' asked Anna, picking up the call.

'We got problems.'

'What's up?'

'Kirsten has been taken. He's smarter than he looks, although I haven't even seen him yet. She's got caught. She's inside what I believe to be a farmhouse and I don't know who I can trust to go in and get her. I need someone with experience, someone who can handle themselves; someone who will not undercut me. Also, I need somebody who can get here quick.'

'You're coming to me for suggestions,' said Anna.

'I'm coming to you because I want you,' said Justin.

'Godfrey has sent me to look for Craig.'

'I need you. I wouldn't call you and tell you this unless it was urgent. She's really in trouble. This isn't some minor group. This isn't the Russians who would hold her, maybe sell her back to us or someone else. These people, they sell bombs, they don't want the hassle—either that or they're anti-establishment. She's working for us. She's one of the establishment. Anna, I need you now.'

'Give me your location,' said Anna.

Justin pressed a button on his phone, waiting for the details to transfer over to Anna Hunt. He could hear some musings on the phone. 'I'll be there,' she said. 'Two hours. Make sure they don't leave with her.'

'Really? There was me going to get my dinner while I was waiting.'

'Two hours, I'll be there.'

Justin went closer to the farmhouse. It was all quiet, and he only cursed slightly when the rain began. Justin positioned himself under a tree, down low in the dark.

The guards rotated. Although you couldn't see weapons in their hands, they definitely were carrying. They kept coming round and round, one after another, looking this way and that, and then, on the hour, they spread out, walking towards him by the tree. Justin quietly stepped behind, then moved behind another one.

He saw the classic patterns, the way they walked. This was a search, which was a methodical one, so much easier to avoid than a random one. It took him ten minutes of dodging this way and that before he ended up back at the tree once again, under shelter as the rain continued to beat down.

There was a tap on his shoulder, and Justin forced himself

not to jump. He looked around to see a weapon pointed at him and then gave a smile. He knew who carried that sort of handgun. Anna Hunt was dressed all in black. Her hair tied up and only a ponytail hanging out from a beanie hat, but her face was blackened.

'You don't seem to be wearing a tactical outfit,' said Anna.

'No,' said Justin. 'I had a go with the hotel trade, but it didn't work.'

Anna pulled a backpack off her shoulders and put it down. She opened the bag.

'Black waterproof trousers in there, black jacket too. You'll find the makeup.'

Justin nodded, thanked her, and then disappeared back, while Anna continued to watch the house. He returned a few minutes later, now clothed all in black, face also fading into the darkness, except for the white eyes.

'Have you confirmed she's in there?'

'No.'

'What's your evidence?'

'She saw Mark Lamb at the gala dinner. The idea was she was going to honey-trap him and take him up to his room. There, she'd knock him out and bring him to me, and we'd haul him back to Godfrey and the rest of you. Everything went well. She got upstairs and then she didn't come out. I went for a pee,' said Justin. 'Probably the best pee I've ever gone for in my life.'

Anna Hunt looked over at him. 'To be fair,' said Justin. 'It was probably the bit after that, which was the best. I had finished what I was doing and was just coming back to the car, and somebody fired a rocket at me. After that, the hotel emptied. I ran round, got into a porter's outfit, ran up the stairs, found the room she was meant to be in. Followed a couple of goons who were leaving it. I pulled them over, convinced them to tell me what was going on, and then ended up here. They said she was in there.'

'You believe them because?'

'Because they're mercenaries. Why die when you can live another day? These people weren't on a cause. They were Mark Lamb's people. These weren't the fundamentalists. These are not the people who are bringing down the organisation.'

'What makes you say that?'

'Too sloppy,' said Justin. 'Way too sloppy. If anybody had been trained like that, you'd have kicked them out by now. I might not know who to trust, but I damn well know one of our own.'

'Good. What makes you think Kirsten was even in that room, though?'

'I found the little phial she was using to drug him. Seemed like she cracked it open at some point. He obviously got to her first, or there were more people or something. They knew she was coming.'

'Was she sloppy?'

'She was quick to do it. Chose to make her way in, rather than wait a couple of weeks because we didn't have the time. He may have suspected that. Outside of that reasoning, no, I don't believe she was sloppy at all.'

'Sounds reasonable then,' said Anna.

'How do we do this?' asked Justin.

Anna looked inside the bag. 'Good old-fashioned way. Find a door, we go in and we just take them out. Seems the obvious thing to me. I think what we need to do, though, is scout the place properly before we go inside. See how much we can find out. I've got the listening gear if I can get up to the wall. Best one of us do it though, while the other sends for the calvary if they don't come back.'

'Fair enough,' said Justin.

'I'll do it,' said Anna. 'I'm more of a field agent than you've ever been. This is not where you excel.'

'That's wholly unfair,' said Justin. 'I'm good at this.'

'But I'm better. You're better in the live field where it's out in the open, people staring at you. You can walk down the street and not be noticed. Here, it's all about stealth, quiet, a little alertness and fitness. I've got that on you. As much as I value your abilities, I'm the one who's better.'

'Fair enough,' said Justin. 'Before you go in there, in case you don't come back, how are you getting on with Craig?'

'Heck of a journey,' she said. 'Traced him all the way down to England, then traced him all the way back. Never found him. His name's been mentioned along with Mark Lamb. The big problem is that on the wind, Mark Lamb is building a large bomb to attack an unknown target, but the name of the monarch has been mentioned. Godfrey is panicking.'

'That's not a word I associate with our boss. Panic. I've never seen him panic.'

'You've never seen his organisation fall apart under his watch,' said Anna. 'He truly doesn't trust anyone. He doesn't even trust me; that's why he's panicking. If he wasn't panicking, he'd know to trust me, he'd know to trust you, he'd know to trust Kirsten.'

'That's one take on it,' said Justin.

'The other being?' asked Anna.

'That he has something to hide.'

'He's Godfrey. He's got everything to hide. Godfrey is the

man who hides everything.'

'No,' said Justin. 'Something real to hide. Something that you would walk away from. And the rest of us. Why are they going after him in the first place? What is this all about?'

Anna went strangely quiet, then she reached inside her bag and took out a small bottle of water. She drank some and handed it over to Justin.

'Thank you,' he said, sipping some down. 'When was the last time you ate?'

'I ate something in the car on the way over,' said Anna. 'Thought this could be long. So, I am fuelled up. I don't suppose you brought back the bag,' said Anna. 'Bars are in the bag.'

Justin reached in and pulled out a bar. It was high in calories and nutrition, although it tasted fairly disgusting. Once he chewed it, he put the rest of it down his throat with a slurp of water. He placed the bottle back in the bag.

'Okay,' said Anna. 'I'll get off and do my scouting. Keep your eyes peeled. I'll be back in—she looked down at her watch—an hour.' Justin looked at his own and nodded, and then watched Anna disappear off into the darkness.

Justin sat for the next hour, watching the building. He had to move, at one point, as the search came out, and then went back again. For the most of it, he was sitting under the tree watching guards potter about. He never saw Anna Hunt once. Wherever she was, she was hidden. He knew she'd taken a device you could put up against the wall, monitor heartbeats as they went past. She had devices that could listen in, too.

The comings and goings kept him on his toes and kept fatigue away, but Justin's mind was running in overtime.

Godfrey was panicked. Godfrey was bothered about something. That wasn't Godfrey. Godfrey was always in charge, but then again, with everyone pulling out from under him or turning tail to someone else, no wonder he was bothered.

Godfrey was a scary individual. He never acted like a tyrant, but he was in a lot of ways. He expected you to do what you were told to do, and if you didn't, he came down hard. Although he always did it with a smile, as if he was doing a favour.

In truth, he didn't like Justin. He knew Justin had too much of an independent mind. He knew he was too clever with computers, and he knew that Anna Hunt rated him. Anna was a quandary for Godfrey. Justin swore the man liked her on more than a professional level. She was loyal to the Service, which is why Justin was wondering if Godfrey had something to hide that was anti-Service. Something that would mean that the wrath of whoever was perpetrating these acts was deserved.

There was a whisper in Justin's ear. 'She's in there,' said Anna's voice. 'She's on the move, going from the east side of the building towards the west. I think it's where the large barn is. Towards the southwest.'

'Is she in imminent danger?'

'Well, it sounds like it. I don't think they're going to execute her. I think they're going to do much worse.'

'Time to move then.'

'Time to move,' said Anna. 'Extreme prejudice.'

'Extreme prejudice? I thought you would just contain and lockdown to find out who these people are?'

'There are people here from the Service,' said Anna. 'If they're not Kirsten, treat them as hostile, extreme prejudice.'

'Okay,' said Justin. He reached inside his jacket and took out his weapon. Extreme prejudice it would be. He'd been hoping it wouldn't be much of a firefight. Anna wasn't so sure.

Chapter 18

Kirsten blinked as the door to her room opened and light flooded in. A click of a switch, and she had to blink repeatedly as the white light invaded her eyes. At first, there was a dark shape in front of her, and then she saw three of them.

'I was just asleep.' It was Emma, still dressed in her outfit from the previous night. Although Kirsten wasn't sure what time of day or night it was. 'I was all for taking you through like you are,' she said. 'But he's not quite like that. He says you need a bit more support, so we're going to let you wear something before you fight.'

Kirsten looked quizzically at her, but the pain her arms were in was forcing her to ignore any jibes pointed towards her. Emma pulled out a gun and pointed it at Kirsten while two men came from behind her and cut the bonds on Kirsten's feet. They then pulled on a pair of knickers before lowering her down, letting her feet touch the floor. They unlocked the handcuffs, and she struggled at first with her arms, but the men pulled a t-shirt on over the top of her head.

'Personally, I think it's because he likes to unveil a prize, and a prize is what you're going to be. Somebody told me you were the darling of the force, that Godfrey particularly liked you. It's probably not a good thing when you come into our company. Take her arms,' said Emma.

Kirsten's arms were pulled behind her while Emma kept the gun trained on her. They were then handcuffed behind and she was prodded forward out of the door. Emma walked behind her while the two men led. They went through a couple of small corridors, then right through a door into what looked like morning light.

The rain was belting down, and she felt it on her skin before a door was opened into a large barn. She was taken to the centre of it and looked around at bales of straw on which sat several men. They looked like fighters. *Operatives*, she thought. They yelled and jeered at her, cat-whistling. One ran up and smacked her on the backside.

'Well, gentlemen. Isn't she worth fighting for? Let's state the rules tonight, shall we? The first man to step forward can fight her on his own, and if he wins, he'll have her. If she wins, she'll fight the next two men together who can have her together if they win. Then the next three men, and by that point, I think there's only four of you left; if she can beat you all, of course, then she'll earn herself another day's respite.'

'I'll take her,' said a man. Clearly, he was the leader of the men on the hay bales, and they cheered for him as he stood up. 'Whatever's left over, I'll leave for you guys.'

Kirsten stood in the ring, looking at the man. He was looking at her like she was some Sunday dinner with gravy, licking his chops. She turned to Emma.

Okay then. If that's how you do it, get the cuffs off. Let's get going.'

'Oh, no,' said Emma. 'The cuffs don't come off.' Kirsten

looked at her. She almost fancied her chances with the cuffs off, despite who these people were. 'Don't worry,' she said, 'because if you get beat, you'll go willingly to them. I have the drugs to make sure of it, and I'm sure they'll willingly show you the best time you've ever had. Certainly, before they dispose of you.'

Emma stepped out of the ring and Kirsten looked over to the corner where someone was standing in shadow. Was that the man who was in before? There were a few other people standing around. Guards. They clearly would not get to be part of the entertainment. She ignored them, focusing on the man opposite.

'Turn away now and I won't kill you,' she said. 'Come for me and I'll kill you.'

'You wish,' he said. 'I'll kill you. I'll bury you, but not until after I have you. Right? Frisky little thing, aren't you? Oh, you'll be good.'

Inside, Kirsten was taking every word the man said, everything they'd just done to her, and channelling it. He would come in confident. She had her arms behind her, and she would seem like a lamb to the slaughter. He may even rush in.

Kirsten stepped forward, leaning, and watched as he came towards her. She was right. He reached forward as if to grab her as if he thought she would be an easy enough to just grab, put to the ground, and do whatever he wanted with her. As he lunged, she stepped to one side, and pivoting on her left foot, she launched her right foot up, catching him right under the chin. The man fell backwards out cold, and Kirsten walked over and drove the base of her foot down on his neck. There was an audible crunch. She stepped back as all of his men went silent.

'Next two,' said Emma. 'If you could put a bit more effort into it, it would be appreciated.'

Kirsten watched two more men stand up, but she saw that they'd been put forward by someone else. One of the other men was obviously the second in command, and he wasn't ready to come at her with just one person to help. Now there were two. She'd have to rethink what she was doing.

'Maybe she'd like a drink, catch her breath before the next round,' said Emma.

Kirsten was hit with a deluge of water from behind. She felt her hair slide down the side of her face, dripping wet. It should have been cold. The barn was cold, but she was too focused, too intense to notice that. Instead, she observed the two men as they circled her. She would need to be quick, always need to be quick.

One man lunged in and Kirsten sidestepped. She went to hit him with a kick to the head, but someone grabbed her from behind. Suddenly she was wrapped up, arms around her mid-rift, pulling her tight. The other man laughed and came towards her, but her legs were still free. Kirsten swung one high and drove it down on top of the man's shoulders. The other followed on top of his head.

She had his neck between her legs, around about her ankles, and she twisted hard. There was a click, and when she let her legs go, the man dropped to the ground. Her own legs came down and round underneath her. The man holding her, somewhat in shock, made the mistake of letting her put her feet on the ground. She bent down quickly, pushing her back up as hard as she could, and lifted the man off the floor.

Her arms were still behind her, but she pushed forward, flipping with him, causing him to land on his back and her to land on top of him. She heard the groan and rolled off, quickly getting back to her feet. As he stood up, she swiped her leg across, catching him on the chin, the next one, catching him on the ribcage, hard. She could hear the break. She continued forward, hitting him time and time again in the face before the last one knocked him completely senseless. Kirsten stepped back into the ring and glared at the men who had been catcalling her, wanting her.

'Just put the bitch down,' said one of them.

'Too tough for you, am I? I thought you said you had real men here,' she said to Emma. 'They can't handle me. They come in pairs and they can't handle me. Three won't be able to handle me either.'

'I think she needs a lesson in doing as she's told, needing to know her place in all of this,' said Emma.

'Not suffering enough for you, am I?' taunted Kirsten. 'Once, they're all dead. I'm coming for you.'

Kirsten wasn't sure quite how wild she looked. That was the impression she wanted to give. The idea that she was some sort of lunatic, and this scheme of playing fair would not work. They'd stick her back in whatever cage, brood about what to do with her. It would buy her time. However, Emma was the problem, and she confirmed it with her next words.

'You are doing well, aren't you? Maybe we'll take the next two on together.'

'I just took two on together,' said Kirsten, 'and I beat them.'

'You did indeed. Let's have the last seven together, the three and the four all together. Go on lads, explain it to her.'

Emma's lipstick shone as she stood beneath one of the stronger beams of light in the shed. Whoever was standing over in the corner in the shadow laughed. Kirsten kept her eyes on the seven men who suddenly stood up. They circled her and she kept spinning around, trying to watch them all.

This would not be easy, but they were scared. Even though there were seven of them, they were actually scared. They'd seen what she'd done to their three colleagues. None of them wanted to be the first to step in. Sure, they might all subdue her, but you wouldn't get your fun with a broken neck.

One lad quickly stepped in and she launched a kick. From behind her, she heard the footsteps of another and spun around to catch him across the chin. He fell back to be caught by two of his colleagues.

'Now, now boys,' she said. 'I might not take all of you, but I think the first four at least will be dead.'

She studied the eyes of those looking at her and was pretty sure that they thought she might be right. Then they started coming in together, all at once. Kirsten picked one, went straight at him, catching him with a knee up to the chin. He fell to the ground, and she drove down with her other knee, planting it into his neck. She wasn't sure if she had got him because she was grabbed. She swung her legs around, catching somebody else. They spun, but then they were on top of her, all of them. She felt hands grabbing her, and she was pushed down to the ground, her hands behind her.

Someone grabbed, held onto her neck, and she could feel her legs being pulled. A knee was planted on her back.

'I'm going to enjoy this,' said Emma suddenly. The men were standing there laughing, jeering at Kirsten, arguing about who was going to have her first. Arguing about how they were going to do it. It was vile, but she'd expected nothing less.

Emma walked over and Kirsten felt a stiletto pushing down into her shoulder. 'Little trollop,' she said, 'little trollop. A dog to be used. Don't think of her as a lady, guys. She's not a quality mare like myself. Have her! Have her in every which way you ever wanted. Do the things you've never been allowed to do, and when you're finished with her, bring her to me and I'll put a bullet in her head.'

Emma bent down in her dress, her knees going into the blood of those Kirsten had beaten earlier. She looked right into Kirsten's eyes.

'It's quite horrific. It's the worst sort of fear,' she said. 'I think it's the worst thing that can happen to you. If you were stronger, you wouldn't let it happen to you, but you're not. You're a dirty little mare on her own. You're someone who has got no one behind them. Godfrey brings in a freelance. Really? Take the money and run, but you'll be getting no money for this. You'll be getting nothing for this.'

Emma stood up, looked at the surrounding men. 'Who's the first, boys?'

One man stepped round behind Kirsten. 'I'll be having her first. Let's see if there's anything left of her for the rest.'

It was clearly the second in command, and Kirsten couldn't see anything behind her. All she knew was there were hands on her legs that she couldn't fight off. As strong as she was, they'd laid her prone on the ground. She had no foundation to work from, nowhere. She tried to prepare herself. She tried to think of escape. There was no way out.

Inside, she shook. Emma was right. One of the greatest fears, one of those things that haunted you. The bullet didn't matter. Getting caught out in a fight didn't matter. But here she was, helpless. Here, about to be a thing to be used.

She heard the cries. She heard the man's belt being unbuckled, and then she heard the bullet fired from a gun.

Chapter 19

Kirsten felt one of her legs coming free. Possibly, the men were trying to stand up. A second gunshot rang out, then a third and a fourth. Kirsten heard men spin, spiral, and cry out. A couple fell across her legs. The one who was holding down her neck suddenly went backwards. Emma spun around on her heels before hitting the floor. There was movement behind her. Kirsten could hear quick feet stepping in and then a voice she recognised.

'You, that wall, now. You with him. Justin, cover the woman. Anyone else alive?'

Kirsten rolled sideways and tried to free herself from those lying on top of her. She guessed they were probably dead and if not, they soon would be. She saw Justin run past before picking up Emma by the neck and throwing her over to presumably where the other prisoners were. He came back towards her, put an arm under her, and helped her up.

Kirsten was still shaking. She had thought this was it. She had thought the genuine horror was going to happen. The adrenaline was ripping through her. She looked over at Anna Hunt. The woman was all in black, face made up, but she knew that voice anywhere.

'Okay?' Anna asked her.

'Yes,' she said.

'Convince me,' said Anna. Kirsten gave her a look, but then walked over to where Emma was clutching her shoulder against the wall. Although she still had her hands handcuffed behind her, Kirsten drove a knee up into the gut of Emma, causing her to double over and then collapse to the ground. Kirsten turned back to Anna Hunt.

'See? I'm fine.'

'Get the cuffs off her, Justin. I've got these guys covered. We'll need to move soon, though. I think we took out everybody else, but just in case.'

'Do you want to find some clothes or something?' said Anna. 'I can sort these people out.'

'Him,' said Kirsten. She went over to the man she'd thought was second in command. 'He's their deputy. The leader's dead. I killed him.'

'Killed him? What were they having you do?' asked Justin.

'Had me fight for my honour. If I killed him, I got the next lot. If I didn't, they got me. That's why I'm dressed like this.'

'Well, go get something on,' said Anna, 'then we'll get out of here.'

'No,' said Kirsten, and marched up to the second in command. He was on his knees, facing the wall, his colleague beside him. Kirsten walked up behind him, drove her knee into the back of the man's head, which smacked off the wall. 'Talk to me,' said Kirsten. 'What's going on? What's this all about?'

'I'll take this,' said Anna.

'No, you won't,' said Kirsten. 'I want to know what's going on. Where's Craig?'

Kirsten felt someone grab her cuffs and pull them backwards.

She found herself walking away from the man and then spun around to see Anna's face.

'I need information,' said Anna, 'and I need it from this lot. I know you think you need it, but you're not in a position to extract it. You're more likely to kill them than to get the information.'

There was a sigh of relief from the second in command, and Anna walked up towards him. 'I'll get it out of you before I kill you. You'll beg me for death, and that's why you'll tell me things, so don't think you're off the hook.'

She clipped him around the back of the head, smacking his forehead into the wall again. She spun over to Emma with her gun.

'Two seconds. Where's the keys to those cuffs or you're dead?'

'My pocket,' said Emma. Anna gave a nod to Justin, who stepped over to the woman, his gun still trained on her, took out the keys, and then uncuffed Kirsten.

'I can handle the three of them. Justin, go make sure she's okay. Find her some clothes from somewhere. We leave in five.'

'You'll never break us in five minutes,' said Emma.

'That's why I'm sending them out,' said Anna. 'They really don't like to watch this.'

Kirsten allowed Justin to help her, and they went out of the shed into the rest of the farmhouse. They found an upstairs room with women's clothes, and Kirsten guessed that this was where Emma had been sleeping. Certainly, there was her scent in the air. She found a pair of jeans, kept her T-shirt on, and then found a pair of boots. It would do for now, and she threw a jacket on too. The woman was taller, so the jeans had to be rolled up. The jacket was slightly big, but the shoes weren't a poor fit at all.

'Thank you,' said Kirsten.

'Not a problem. I wasn't sure who to trust, so I went and got Anna. She's a lot of things, but she wants the good of the Service. She wants the good of the country, and she respects you. Anna doesn't abandon her people.'

'No, she doesn't, but I think she's worried. She's not sure what Godfrey's up to.'

'I'm not sure what Godfrey's up to. Those men in there, they're from the Service. I know several of them. They're openly in rebellion. How many did you take out?' asked Justin.

'Three, maybe four. I took out their leader, the first one, then a pair. I took them out, and I think I got someone before they held me down. Really, Justin, thank you. That's truly one thing I fear.'

'I don't blame you,' he said. 'Also, not the way we behave. They do a lot of the dirty operations. Quite brutal. I think it's built into them. Godfrey once said to me he didn't like them, but he had to use them for what they did. I didn't think that was any excuse, but you follow orders, do what you do.'

'That's why I got out. Freelance. Pick what I want to do, how I want to do it.'

'You didn't pick this, though. Anna's got an update on Craig. She'll tell you. Things aren't looking good.'

Kirsten walked back with Justin towards the shed. As they approached the door, they heard men screaming.

'Shall we give her a minute?' asked Justin. The rain was still pouring down, so the pair of them went to a small alcove set in a wall, which had a roof extending out over it.

'You not cold?' said Justin. 'I'm freezing. I was standing out there for ages, waiting for Anna to get here.'

'Cold. They hung me up in there for a couple of hours at least, if not more. It was cold. Nothing on. Hanging from my own hands. I know Craig's not here. He wouldn't let that happen to me. He wouldn't.'

'You're thinking of who Craig was. You don't know who Craig is now.'

'But I'll find him. I'll bring him back.'

'He may not come back. And with what Anna's been saying, he's gone quite far. Way too far.'

'You don't know that. We won't know that until I speak to him. He'll listen to me. He'll—'

'Kirsten,' said Justin. He moved in front of her, taking himself out of the alcove, letting the rain fall on him so he could look into her eyes. 'I more than anyone would love you to be back with him; would love him to be the way he was. I still blame myself for what happened. It was I who pulled the trigger. I blew that boat up. He lost his legs because of me.'

'No,' said Kirsten. 'He would've been in a Russian jail. He'd have died horribly if it wasn't for you. We didn't get him in time. That was the problem. All of us. The Russians did it to him. They took him. Godfrey is more responsible for this than anyone on our side.'

'Maybe,' said Justin. He grabbed both her shoulders with his hands and earnestly looked at her. 'Listen, I think he's gone. I think it's too far. Whether it's the trauma, the pain, whether it's the fact he lost his legs, whatever the hell it is, he's gone. It's too far. I don't want to see you waste your life on trying to bring him back when he's not there to be brought back. Kirsten, trust me, you may find him. You may have to put a bullet in him. This is not a path you want to do. It's a path for

Anna. It's a path for someone else. Let me do it.'

'It's not what you do. It's not the way you work,' said Kirsten. 'I can't walk away from this, Justin. Do you understand me? I can't walk away. It's not like not Dom and Carrie-Anne, heading off together into the sunset. I tried to do that with Craig.

'We were out. We were clear, and it came back at us, the past. I can't walk away this time because the past will come back at me with someone new. I need to find Craig. Look Justin, I need to know. I need to see if I can bring him back, and if I can't, then maybe I'll have to put a bullet in him.'

'And you think you're strong enough to do that?' asked Justin.

'I better be, or he might put one in me,' she said.

'Walk,' said Justin. 'Walk.'

'No,' said Kirsten. 'I know what you're saying is right. I know you're only thinking of me and you're protecting me, but this is the man I chose. I can't leave him. Whatever he has become, it's not his fault.'

'And it's not yours either.'

'I'm doing it. Don't ask me again. Don't talk to me about it in that way again, please.'

Justin nodded and turned away, but Kirsten tapped him on the shoulder. 'Thank you for trying. Somebody needed to try. Godfrey's using me. I'm not sure about Anna.'

'Anna would be too scared to ask you to walk away. Maybe she would just think it'd not be worth her time and effort. She won't want you off focus.'

Kirsten stepped forward and hugged Justin. 'Ever since I went into this, ever since you came into the team, you've been a friend,' she said. 'I don't call many people friends in this business. You are.'

'And Anna will be as well.'

'And is that it? Is that what we've got at the moment, the three of us?'

'Unless you're going to get Dom and Carrie-Anne back.'

'They're gone. They're out. I'm never bringing them back.'

Together the pair walked through the rain back to the shed where they opened the door and found Anna Hunt sitting on a straw bale.

'There's an imminent problem,' said Anna. 'From what they've just told me, it really is a problem. I need to go. I traced Craig down to England. And then I tracked him back up to Scotland. His name's been mentioned by that of Mark Lamb. I think he is working with Lamb as part of the growing discord with the Service. This rebellion, this anti-Service, they're bigger than we think. They're throughout the organisation. Godfrey has panicked. I have never seen Godfrey panicked in all of my career,' said Anna.

'He stood up to you after you nearly lost Craig and he didn't bat an eyelid. Godfrey does not flinch. It's like he's almost running. He's panicked. We need to stop the attack that's imminent.'

'Okay,' said Kirsten, 'but I think the first thing we need to do is to get the hell out of here, and I could do with a shower and a sleep. My arms are still hurting. And, well—'

'Come on,' said Anna. She put her arm around Kirsten, something she'd never done before.

'Has it ever happened to you?' said Kirsten.

'It's been tried. The disappointing thing is that the four of them were not around to tell others not to try it.' Kirsten looked up at Anna and gave a faint smile. 'I'm glad I was here for you.'

Together, the three of them disappeared out of the farm-house, through the countryside to where Anna had her car. She drove them back to Kirsten's flat. It was daytime, but Kirsten drew the curtains and Anna took the sofa. Justin lay down on the floor, a couple of pillows under his head, and Kirsten hit the shower.

As she stood there washing herself down, she suddenly trembled. Her legs buckled. She collapsed in the shower and tears flowed. It had been so close, so damn close. Her body juddered. Wave upon wave of terror suddenly came back at her, and then arms were around her. She looked up and saw the face of Anna Hunt holding her tight in the shower.

'It'll get better,' she said. 'They didn't. It will get better, but it won't go.' Kirsten nodded and allowed herself to be held as the water continued to fall.

Chapter 20

It was early afternoon when everyone awoke in Kirsten's flat. She noticed Anna Hunt staring at her, watching her consistently throughout the time she was making breakfast. Kirsten would have liked to have turned round and said she was fine, no problems at all. The physical trauma she received was nothing. She'd only been held as she had been many times before. This time, the imminent threat had damaged her psychologically. She knew she woke up three times. Nightmares, and not just the evil monsters, nightmares about—well, she didn't want to think about that. *Make the food*, she told herself. *Make the food. Get on.*

Justin Chivers was busying himself on his phone, organising flights.

'So, the two of you are heading for London?' asked Kirsten.

'Yes,' said Anna. 'There's an attack imminent on the Monarch. I can't stay here and go after Craig. I need to protect our sovereign. If I didn't, Godfrey would have me hauled up. Sovereign's our boss. If they were to get past the Service and carry out the attack, well, they'll send a statement. Not a good one.'

'So, I'm going back with her,' said Justin.

'But you could stay with me,' said Kirsten. 'I could really use your help in finding Craig, in finding Mark Lamb.'

'Mark Lamb's just a bomber. He only makes the devices, he doesn't plant them. I would suspect he isn't far off completing his work, passing on what he needs to give.'

'I guess so,' said Kirsten.

Anna Hunt walked over to where Kirsten was slicing a cucumber. She didn't stand at a distance, but wrapped her arms around the woman like a mother.

'You're afraid to be left alone, not because of Craig, not because of Mark Lamb, but because of what happened. I don't blame you. You could do with being with good people. You could do with time off. We don't have it,' said Anna.

'I need to be in London. I'd say come with me, but you need to resolve this with Craig as well. That's where it's all going. If the Service is falling and he's in it, and you think you can bring him back out, you'll need to do it, but you'll also need to make him run. Godfrey won't forgive.'

'Would you?' asked Kirsten?

'It would depend on a lot. I would need to see what he's done. It would depend if he's still a threat.'

'It could put you against me, then, if that's the case.'

'I like to think of myself as a friend,' said Anna, 'but I'm a true professional. I'm working for the Service, to protect the Service. I protect the country. That's at the top of my agenda, the country. That's why I do this.'

'And if the Service is corrupt?' asked Kirsten.

'The Service will need to be sorted,' said Anna. 'Look, Kirsten, I don't know what's coming in the days ahead, but you didn't take this for a job. You didn't take this for the money. This was to find Craig. You need to resolve that. Maybe when that's done, you can get some time away and you can heal from what happened last night. If there's anything in that regard, I will help.'

'What are you going to do in London?' asked Kirsten.

'I've got a name. I've got a name who's in London. One of the Service. I'm going to find them and I'm going to bring this to a conclusion as best I can.'

Kirsten turned around, put her arms around Anna, and hugged her. 'Stay safe,' she said. 'Look after him, too. Thank you for coming. Without you—'

'Don't think about that. They didn't. Be grateful, be thankful, and work through the terror. It's a pity you left,' said Anna. 'We made a good team, you and me. I always knew you would. I always knew you'd be a piece of conscience for me. Someone who would challenge. Godfrey never wanted you in. Godfrey didn't like you, but I've said it before—screw Godfrey. It's coming home to roost for him now.'

Anna disappeared quickly. Kirsten thought she almost saw a tear in the woman. She looked over at Justin as Anna entered the bathroom.

'She okay?'

'She once—well, once is maybe the wrong word. Her and Godfrey, there's been something running between them for a long time. It's probably her weakness, if she has one. She knows what he's like. She knows the things he's done, and they don't sit well with her. Anna will take someone down if it needs done. Anna will show very little mercy if very little mercy is required, but she's also someone who plays with a very straight bat.

'If she doesn't need to despatch someone, she won't. If she doesn't need to destroy something, she won't. Godfrey will hold secrets. Anna will not sacrifice people but will make the hard call if they need to die in furthering the cause, furthering what we're doing. If it's necessary to put them in harm's way, she'll do it. Godfrey will just have people dispatched. He will lose his people to advance his own aims. He will sacrifice. Anna's never sacrificed. She'll always give them a fighting chance if that hard call has to be made. I think she loves him, and she hates him at the same time.'

'Well, you take care of yourself down there. Leave the ladies alone.'

Justin laughed. 'I'll do my best. I can't believe I can still keep that rumour going.' He gave Kirsten a hug.

'Thanks for coming after me,' she said. 'Thank you for getting her and not just getting yourself killed in the process.'

'If she hadn't been there, it was Dom and Carrie, and then I don't know what I was going to do. But we got you. Stay safe.'

Anna Hunt reemerged from the bathroom, having wiped down her eyes. 'Let's eat,' she said. 'We've got a flight to catch. You can drop us off in the car.'

'What's happening with yours?'

'Someone will pick it up. I'm not driving to London. There won't be time.'

The three of them sat down to lunch, prepared by Kirsten. There was nothing grand about it, and for the most of it, they sat in silence. When it came the time to take them to the airport, Kirsten drove them in her car, round to the rear of Inverness, before driving out onto one of the private aprons. A small jet was there, and Anna Hunt told her to stay in the car.

'Find him, find out if he's still recoverable. If he's not, don't hesitate.' Kirsten looked over at her. 'I mean it, don't hesitate, because if you do, he won't. I've seen people go bad before. I've seen what people can become.'

'Are you talking about Godfrey, because you haven't put him down?'

'Godfrey's our boss,' said Anna, 'And when he's done, he's still fighting for this country; he just fights differently. It's a bit more complicated than someone who's turned against us.'

'Is it? I'm not sure it is.'

'You think it's simple with Godfrey?'

'It's not what I meant,' said Kirsten. 'It's complicated with Craig.'

Anna put her hand over onto Kirsten's as it held on to the steering wheel. 'I've grown to trust you. I've grown to let you make your decisions; make a good one. Come on,' she said to Justin in the rear. 'Let the girl get to it. We'll catch up soon. Tell me if you find anything. Tell me how it goes.'

Kirsten gave a nod, and once they'd cleared the vehicle, drove back out on the Inverness roads, returning to her flat.

She parked up in the street, climbed out, and made her way up towards the front door. As she did so, she felt an unease. Kirsten rebuked herself. *An operative needed to be calm, needed to be steady, needed to observe all around them. You couldn't do that when you got yourself tensed up about nothing, because there were no facts or evidence to be tensed up with at the moment. Relax, scan, survey, do all that*, she thought.

She approached the front door of her flat, took out her key, and opened it. There was nothing unusual about the flat. When she closed the door behind her, she felt a chill. Her mind flashed back, her legs held down, her neck held down. Someone's behind her, laughs, a single gunshot. She almost jumped when she heard it in her mind. If it hadn't had been . .

163

'Enough,' she said to herself. Kirsten needed to think, but she also felt anxious. She wanted a bath, but she had a shower. She went in and stood in the shower for the next twenty minutes letting the water caress over her. Slowly, the muscles relaxed. Her mind eased, and that's when she spotted it. It was a bar of soap. Kirsten used gel. She washed her body with gel. There was shampoo up above, but here was soap. There was only one person who had ever used soap in her shower. She tensed, then she left the shower running.

Craig used that soap, she thought. She opened the door of the shower and stepped out. She grabbed a towel, a large one, and wrapped it around her. Slowly, she opened the door and peered out into the rest of the flat. There was no one in the living area. She walked around looking into the kitchen part—, no one there either.

Slowly, she stalked her way over to the bedroom, taking a gun out from underneath the sofa. There was no one in there either. She walked over to the windows, closed all the curtains, before sitting down on the sofa. The shower was still running, but she wanted to think. She stood up, turned, and walked back into the shower, switching it off, and then dried herself.

Kirsten put on a dressing gown and re-entered the living area of her flat. There were a few papers on the coffee table because Justin had been scanning them. There was a rack beside the table that had early papers and some magazines. One sitting in the middle was new. It was thick; it was a weapons magazine. Craig used that one.

Kirsten's heart thumped. Part of her was going into a joy. He was about; he had made contact. Another part of her was wondering what was going on. Why do this? Why play? Why show her he could invade what was now her space? After all, he had left; he'd abandoned her. Therefore, the flat was hers, where she lived now.

Had he put cameras in? Would he be watching her? The previous night came back at her again, when they toyed with her, when they'd looked to use her. Kirsten felt chilled. She sat on the sofa, arms wrapped around herself, cursing herself for not being able to think more rationally.

She walked through to her bedroom, and then she noticed, it was creased. The sheets on one side were creased. She never slept on that side, that was Craig's side. Kirsten walked over and thought she saw something peering out from underneath one pillow. She reached and took it; it was an envelope. She walked back to the sofa and sat down.

If he'd come to kill her, she'd be dead. If he'd come to talk, he'd be there. He'd come to give a message, or maybe she just wanted—*Well*, she thought, *let's find out what he wants.*

She opened the envelope, praying it would say he'd done a runner, gone off to some foreign country. She would follow him then, follow him and talk to him, set up a life somewhere else, a life where they could be together.

Kirsten, it read, *Kessock Bridge, midnight. I think we need to talk. Craig.*

Kirsten stared at the letter. What was this? Was this him coming back to her? Was this him trying to take her with him to whatever fancy he was on, or was he just lost? What was going on? She really didn't know, but looking at it, the one thing she knew was that she couldn't not go. She'd go alone. Kirsten would give him a chance to explain, give him a chance to be a part of her again.

She sat back on the sofa, the letter on her lap, not sure

whether to cry or whether to be angry at him. If she cried, would it be tears of joy or tears of sadness? She glanced at the clock and felt the next hours before midnight would be the longest of her life.

Chapter 21

Kirsten felt sick in her stomach as she left the flat that night, getting into her car and driving towards the Kessock Bridge. She had come from the Inverness side, but she wanted to scout the whole bridge before parking the car. Passing the football club to drive over the bridge, she parked up where the tourists can view the dolphins.

She walked back along, dressed in her black jacket, black jeans, and boots. She let her hair hang out instead of wrapping it up. Craig needed to see her, not the trained operative. He had fallen for her after all, not what she was. She'd given all that up when she went to Zante with him. But you can't leave the Service.

She'd heard that before too many times, and, it appeared it came after her. Godfrey's mistake. Godfrey's dirty deed, when he tried to swap captives, but killed his enemy's operative, anyway. It cost Craig his legs and possibly changed her man's allegiances.

As she walked to the bridge, the rain fell down. The wind whipped along, but the cold she felt came from inside. She tried to walk steadily. Tried not to show any apprehension, but who was she kidding? She walked to the middle of the

Kessock Bridge, and watched the traffic passing by. Kirsten was exposed, in the open, and if a car came past, the window could come down, and they could kill her right there and then.

She didn't believe Craig would do that. She thought there was still something in him, something that wanted her. After all, why bother with this? He'd been in the flat. He could've just waited and killed her there. Did he even have permission to do this? After all, she'd been captured, and they were going to—oh yes, they were going to do that, weren't they?

Had Craig known about that? Was it the same people? How deep was he actually involved in this, if indeed he was? What did it mean he'd gone rogue? Anna had never fully explained because there was no concrete proof. It was a rumour; it was hearsay.

Kirsten stood with her hands on the railings, looking out towards the lights of Inverness. When she looked back down towards the Inverness side of the bridge, she saw a figure wheeling himself up. Craig had always been so tall and strong in how he walked. Kirsten was never a tall woman. Short, but stocky, well built, but he was always that bit taller until he lost his legs. Until he'd gone to the chair, and then every time they were together, she was towering above him. She'd hated that; so had he.

As he got closer, Kirsten stood watching him. It was the same face, which was now getting soaked in the rain, for he had no hat on. He had a jacket, but his trousers were getting soaked.

'I hoped you'd come,' he said.

'You ran when I wasn't there. You disappeared. I was coming back for you.'

'Anna Hunt came after me. Did you send her?'

'I wasn't well, nearly died. I had to save London.'

'We left the Service,' said Craig. 'We left it. Now you're back. Now you're back serving Godfrey.'

'I serve myself. They pay me. I pick what jobs I do.'

'And yet you're here,' he said bitterly.

'I've come after you, for me. I want to know who's still there. Craig, I want to know what I lost, that they just didn't blow that boat up.'

She turned away and looked out towards Inverness. 'Am I here for any good reason?' she said. 'Is there anything of you in there?'

'You need to listen,' he said. 'There's something rotten at the core. The Service is tainted. Godfrey is the worst of it. The Service is corrupted. People have turned.'

'The Service is corrupted? I was caught. These people who are standing away from the corrupted Service caught me.'

She turned and stared at him, examining his face. 'You knew that as well, didn't you? You knew.'

'I know now,' he said. 'I didn't know then. I didn't know.'

'What? That they planned to have their way with me? If it hadn't had been for Anna and Justin, I'd have been on the floor of that shed. They'd have killed me, but killed me in the worst way. That's your so-called people. That's your so-called justice.'

'It's wrong. I would've killed them. I wouldn't have let them do that to you. The Service is worse than even that. Godfrey is.'

'Then show me some proof,' said Kirsten. 'Show me some proof. I'll take it to Anna. To Justin. I'll show the lot of them. What is your proof?'

'I can't give that over. I can't reveal the stuff that I know. We can't do that. You'll know where it's come from. People will be—'

'People will stand in the light. It'll all be done in the way Godfrey does it.'

'You're justifying his actions. You're standing for him, are you?'

Kirsten walked forward and knelt down on the pavement, the water seeping in through her jeans. She reached forward with her hands, taking Craig's face.

'I do not work for him. I work for myself and I can walk away anytime.'

'Of course, you work for him. Of course, you—'

Kristen continued to hold his face, stroking the side of it gently.

'Let's go,' she said, 'like we planned, like we did in Zante. Go somewhere, anywhere, just the two of us together. You could love me again. I could be your woman. We could just enjoy every day together. I don't care that you can't walk. All of that's irrelevant,' said Kirsten. 'The man I knew is still in there. I know you are.'

She reached forward and kissed him on his lips, but he didn't respond. She stepped back away from him.

'You need to join with us. Gethsemane is going to bring about a new order within the Service. A new order.'

'You're following someone who's bringing down the Service. The Service protects the country.'

'Bullshit,' said Craig. 'It protects no one. Godfrey doesn't protect the country.'

'I damn well protect the country. Anna protects the country. There are many good people out there who protect the country. I stopped a bomb in London. Twice,' she said. 'I've stopped other things. People who couldn't defend themselves. Come to their rescue. It's what I do. This is why I joined.'

'And above that game, Godfrey plays a different one. Godfrey plays something else,' said Craig. Kirsten stared at the anger on his face. She could see his hands, tensed.

'You need to come to my side,' he said. 'Follow Gethsemane. He'll show you the way. He's vowed to attack the head of the Service. Vowed to bring it down. Come join us,' said Craig. 'We could do with you. There's no better operative. Maybe Anna, but you could do so much good. You could do—'

'Craig, they held me on the floor. They were going to—'

Tears streamed down Kirsten's face. This was not how you did it as an operative. This was not how you conducted yourself, but this was Craig. Her heart was being pulled this way and that. Part of her wanted to believe him. Part of her wanted to see that he was actually being the genuine person in all this. He was doing this out of a just cause, one she could jump on board with, but she couldn't. He was almost defending the very people who had tried to take away her own womanhood, to destroy something so precious.

'Damn it, Craig. Give me evidence. Show me. Give me something. Give me something and I can come to you if you will not come to me. Or else screw them all, screw them all, and let's get out of here. Am I not enough?'

She watched him stare at her. 'It's gone beyond us,' he said. 'It's gone well beyond us. Gethsemane requires that it's all brought down. It's all changed. Godfrey will go; Anna will go if she stands with him. The rest of them, one by one, we're finding them. One by one, they'll be challenged. The good ones, they'll have time to join. That's why I'm here.'

Kirsten turned away from him. Then she spun back, running

up to him, kneeling down. She took his face in her hands.

'Craig, damn well listen to yourself. You've been given a chance. They weren't giving me a chance. Not even just going to despatch me. They wanted to abuse. They wanted to take everything from me before leaving me to die. That's your so-called friends. That's this revolution you're in.

'You know me. You know I don't back a side that does stuff like that. I don't back Godfrey; that's why the hell I left, and you should leave with me. We need to go back to Zante. Back to when it was us. We need to start again. I'll walk, but not for Gethsemane. I'll walk for you.'

'Look at me,' he said. 'Look at me. I can't physically walk away, and I can't walk away knowing what I know.'

'What the hell do you know then? Tell me. Tell me.'

'It will compromise people. Too many people.'

'Don't you trust me?' She screamed at him. 'This is me, Kirsten. We were everything. We knew the ins and outs of each other. Just tell me. Trust me and tell me. If it's so compelling, I'm with you. You know I will be. Tell me. Tell me now, Craig.'

She watched his hand reach inside his jacket. He pulled out a gun, holding it at her. It was kept low in the seat, so passing cars couldn't see.

'Step back and away. Give me an answer.'

'Then what? Give you the wrong one and you kill me? You bring me here, what, to kill me? I came here because I love you. Do you still love me? Do you still want me? Above all this shit? Tell me, do you really?'

Almost automatically, Kirsten took a tracking device and subtlety placed it on Craig's wheelchair.

Craig's face was impassive. 'Gethsemane is offering you an opportunity. Are you going to take it?'

'You won't tell me. You won't show me what you know. Won't trust me,' said Kirsten, tears streaming down her face. 'It's not something I can do.'

He nodded, putting the gun back inside, and reached down for the wheels of his chair.

'If we see each other again, we'll be enemies. I won't show any restraint.'

She stood, tears streaming down her face, watching as he carefully turned his wheelchair around and started wheeling himself away from her. She stared as he made the long trip to the bottom of the bridge and the small lay-by there. A van pulled up inside of it, and he was helped into it. The van then drove up to the bridge.

Kirsten stood looking at it, wondering if someone would take a shot at her from inside. They had her answer, after all. The van just pulled past and drove off north.

Kirsten was soaked through. Physically cold. Emotionally numb. She felt broken. She walked back to her car. *Who was Gethsemane?* she thought. *Who was this person who had so engaged Craig, so taken him on board?* He'd spurned her. She'd given it all up for him. They'd gone. They'd been together. They'd been each other in Zante.

Godfrey had caused the rupture. Godfrey and his dealings—his messing—had caused her to lose her man. He would answer. He would answer for this mess he'd created. This destruction that was going on within the Service.

She had to understand it; she had to see it through. Walking away was an option. She could disappear out of the whole fight, and probably nobody would come after her. Maybe one day, but not for a long while. If Godfrey had caused all this, then Godfrey would be the one to pay, but she needed to know what was happening. If somebody had turned Craig against her, then Gethsemane would pay as well. How did she find Gethsemane? She pondered, trudging back to her car.

When she reached out to open the car door, she knew she had her answer. Godfrey. Godfrey was the one to find out. And if he couldn't, to meet Craig again, and draw it from him.

Chapter 22

Kirsten called the Service demanding to see Godfrey and was told that Godfrey was not available. So, she called Anna Hunt—said she needed to see Godfrey. Anna asked why, and Kirsten said she just needed to, that she would tell her afterwards. Anna wasn't happy about that, but when Kirsten said to trust her, she did it straight away.

Godfrey arrived in a jet at Inverness airport and never got off the plane. Kirsten drove onto the apron, stepped out of her car, and walked over to the aircraft steps, which were guarded by two rather large men at the top. As soon as she was on board, Kirsten was invited to sit in a seat opposite Godfrey, and the jet closed up. Kirsten went to ask Godfrey something, sitting in his dapper suit and tie, but he held up his hand. The jet taxied out, causing Kirsten some consternation for a moment, but Godfrey held up his hand again.

'It's okay, my dear. I just didn't like the thought of sitting around on an apron at the moment. Too easy to be attacked. Mr Chivers was attacked with a rocket launcher. Our enemies are quite happy to play with rather large destructive forces. They won't be too picky about who gets hurt.'

Kirsten sat back until the jet took off and left the mainland.

'We'll orbit out here somewhere,' said Godfrey, 'till our discussion's done. Now, what is so important that you have me fly all the way here?'

'I need to know . . . who is Gethsemane?'

Godfrey waved at those around him in the cabin and they disappeared into the rear section. He unclipped his belt and sat forward, elbows on the table. *Not like him,* she thought. *Not like him at all.*

'I do not know of a Gethsemane,' he said. 'Where did you hear it?'

'Craig reached out to me,' she said. 'I met him on the Kessock Bridge. You can check the CCTV if you want. At one point, he pulled a gun on me, but he asked me to join Gethsemane. He said you were bringing down the Service. He said you were the problem. You were the cause. He said Gethsemane was going to deal with you.'

'And did you? Is that why you're here?'

'No,' said Kirsten. 'He backed the side that the previous night before meeting him had looked to—'

'Yes, I heard,' said Godfrey quickly. 'I heard, and I'm sorry. It's a weapon that many people don't think of. A weapon still used. Torture almost seems simpler than a weapon like that. People recover from torture better than that.'

'Well, thankfully, because of Anna and Mr Chivers, I didn't have to recover,' lied Kirsten. 'Who is Gethsemane?'

'I don't know,' said Godfrey. He sat back in his seat.

'Liar,' said Kirsten, 'Who is Gethsemane? Craig wouldn't tell me. Now, you won't tell me. Who is he?'

'I don't know. I don't even know if it's a he or a thing or a what. Literally, I do not know.'

'He didn't tell me much else, but he turned down my offer

176

to run.'

'You were going to run?' said Godfrey. It seemed to catch him a little off guard.

'Of course,' said Kirsten. 'I'm on your pay. I'm not in your Service. I can hightail out of here. Have taken him away from all of this.'

'But you can never leave the Service,' said Godfrey. 'Even those who quit.'

'I'd rather run that way than deal with the rubbish we're in at the moment.' She unhooked her seat belt, stood up, and began pacing inside the small aircraft. There wasn't a lot of room.

'Did you let him get away?' asked Godfrey. 'Did you let him just walk away from you?'

'And what if I had? What if I had?'

'You're in my employ. I want him.'

'I've traced him. There's a tracker on him. I will go to him again.'

'Gethsemane, whoever this is or what it is, I believe intends to attack the monarch. We have that imminent, so go to Craig and find out as much information as you can. Beat it out of him if you have to. Remember, his sort were prepared to do much worse to you than I can.'

'You don't speak to me like that,' said Kirsten. 'I can walk from this, and if you come after me, I'll leave a trail, a trail of blood back to you. You put Craig where he was, so don't you ever tell me to kill him. If he has to be put down, it'll be for my reasons, my judgment, not yours.'

'I have a matter to attend to,' said Godfrey. 'From now on, contact Anna. Don't contact me! Dragging me all the way up here for a name.'

'Dragging you up to confirm who this is. You thought you

knew, didn't you?'

'I do not know what you speak of, but Gethsemane is a new contact, one we can look into, so I thank you for that.'

He reached over and pressed a button beside the table and a steward came in. 'Tell our pilot we're happy to land again. Miss Stewart will be getting off.' He turned back to Kirsten. 'Take your seat, my dear. You never know when things go wrong when you land. Always better to be buckled in.'

Ten minutes later, Kirsten was walking off the plane and back to her car. She didn't look back as the plane taxied back out. Kirsten checked her phone for where the tracker that she'd put on Craig's wheelchair was. The device was small, but it would be found eventually. She saw it was at a farmhouse outside of Inverness. It made sense to be outside, especially with the numbers of people they were talking about. The Service was also used to using these types of buildings, so those within this rogue group would be used to them. Indeed, some of them may have been there.

She got into the car and drove close to where the farmhouse was, but it was too bright and she went home for the rest of the evening. Her dreams were fitful and involved men she didn't like, but when she woke up, she at least felt rested.

Dressing up, and blacking her face, Kirsten headed back out to the farmhouse where the tracker had ended. She crept in close to the surrounding bushes. There weren't many patrolling but she would have to be careful. The night was dark, many clouds in the air, but there was no rain.

Kirsten wished there had been because rain ate up the noise. Still, she could be quiet and she crept up towards the farmhouse building. The guards were patrolling, walking around every five minutes, but she sought the best place to enter. She waited out in the dark until she saw the lights of the house go out.

How many were in there? Where did they group? Did they have dorms? She wasn't sure what she was going in for, either. She'd see. Maybe she could get photographs of everyone. Maybe she could understand who was on the other side.

Once everything had settled down, it was nearly three in the morning. Kirsten waited for a patrol to go past and made her way quickly over to a rear door. The lock wasn't difficult to pick, and as she stepped inside, she scanned for cameras. There were none. Too much wiring, too much detail made people suspicious, and yet here we had a safe house that seemed full.

It wasn't normal. You would have a couple of people because from the outside, you wouldn't be able to see them, but they had patrolling guards. They'd obviously made this a base. The other problem with cameras was they always told who was there. They were a record, especially if anything was taped. Difficult to erase if somebody else could tap in. Technology was too good these days. The old-school methods sometimes worked the best.

Once inside, Kirsten found herself in a hallway. She crabbed along. There were snores coming from the room beside her, and slowly, she turned the door handle. There was no light from inside. When she peered in, she saw a man on a sofa snoring. She closed the door gently.

In the front room, there were empty glasses and pizza boxes too. She crept her way upstairs. It looked like there were three rooms. She opened one and found it to be overstocked with makeshift beds. People were lying all over the floor. There must have been at least ten people in here.

Kirsten closed the door again and crept to the next one. There was someone lying on the floor. It was Craig. He was turned away from her, but the legs were missing. Also in the room were several other men. Kirsten stepped back out of the room and checked the third one.

Here, women were sleeping, and she thought she may have seen one of them before down in London. She hadn't spoken to her, just been in and about the office when Kirsten had visited previously. Kirsten looked down and noticed a few pads and documents sitting in a bag. She took them out, and with her small camera, she began photographing them. Slowly, she put them back and exited the room. Everywhere had just been about bedding down. There was only this one pile of records that she'd seen. Maybe most things were being kept in their heads.

That was always the safest way. She was going to creep out when she opened the door and stepped into the room Craig occupied again. She drew close to him, bent down so close she could hear him breathe.

What are you? she thought to herself. *What have you done? Where are you at with this?* She wanted to grab him, pick him up and run him out of the place, but with her last conversation, she knew that wasn't an option. Slowly, she stood up, backing her way out, but as she went to, a light came on in the hall outside.

Kirsten moved herself to the edge of the room, avoiding the bodies on the floor. They were still snoring away. They came closer to the room and she could hear them opening the door of the room beside them. *Were they checking? Were they worried about having seen something? How would she get out?*

She looked left and right. She couldn't do the windows here.

180

There wouldn't be enough time. She had an idea. Quickly, she took off her trousers and stood beside the door. As she heard others come up towards it, she cracked it and left her leg outside.

'There's no one in here,' she whispered. 'We're in the middle of something. If you don't want to feel Craig's wrath, I think you need to pass this one by.'

'Dirty sod,' said the guy. 'We'll just come in and check.'

'I've got nothing on,' said Kirsten, harshly, but quietly. 'You are not waking up this room when I'm standing here starkers. Go away, let me get on with this.'

The two men discussed something quickly, Kirsten ready to attack them if they came in.

'Ten minutes,' they said. 'Ten minutes and get back to the other room and then we'll come in and check again.'

'Something up?' she asked.

'Thought they saw something outside. Wanted us to check.'

'Make it five minutes,' said Kirsten then. 'But I'll get grumpy if you're not back.'

'Cheers,' said the man. 'Five minutes. I hope he's quick for you.'

Kirsten closed the door and quickly put on her trousers. Two minutes later, she'd opened it and was coming back down the corridor. The soldiers had gone down the stairs and could be heard in the living room. She swept past the open door quickly and didn't wait to wonder if they'd hear, instead making for the back door.

If the guard was inside, she should be okay outside, and if she wasn't, she would fire. Quickly, she opened the back door, saw no one, and disappeared off into the dark.

Kirsten had something with her; she knew where they were.

She had to talk to Justin, discover what these notes were that she'd photographed, see if they led anywhere. If they did, there was no point in disturbing them. But if they didn't, she'd come back with a bigger squad and take these people in, including Craig.

As she drove off in the car, Craig's face came back to her, lying there with all these people. All those people who had left the Service turned on it, and yet she still didn't know who Gethsemane was. She swore Godfrey lied to her face. Not that it shocked her, but she needed to know who this man was that Craig had put his trust in. Craig wasn't a light-hearted man. He had convictions, but maybe the battering he had taken had made those convictions go askew. She would find out. She would know who was Gethsemane.

Chapter 23

Kirsten sat in her house sending the photographs she'd taken over a secure line to Justin Chivers. There was a cipher on the note she'd photographed. One she couldn't break herself. Justin Chivers had expertise in these matters. He would soon do it. She was sure of that. Meanwhile, she paced the floor.

She'd made herself a coffee, but hadn't sat down to drink it, instead going back and forward, sipping from the mug until it was empty. Then she made another one, then another one. Next, she forced herself to have a shower. Then she came and sat back down, put on the television, but there was nothing of interest on. What could be of interest? This was everything.

Breaking the cipher might show what they were involved in. Craig was clearly hanging out with the people who were attacking the Service. He was there in the middle of it, and he must've been offering them something. After all, he had no legs. You'd have to transport him everywhere. Somebody would've had to carry him up those farmhouse steps to the upper floor, or did he carry himself about on his hands only? Possibly. He'd always been determined when she knew him before the incident.

Kirsten stood up again and went to the drawn curtains at her windows. She looked out down at the street below. There was nothing. Nobody. Did they know she was in? If they did, maybe they would come after her. She hadn't gone into hiding. She was now back in her own flat. Maybe she was just hoping he would make contact again.

She was a little uneasy, though, wondering just who Craig was now. It seemed he was gone, seemed that he was tied in with the fate of those who had subverted the Service. The days ahead would be complicated, she believed. They would be quite strange. She was thankful she had Anna and Justin, at least whom she trusted. She could at least trust Anna to do the right thing in terms of the country. The two of them would pull her through if they could.

Her mobile phone rang, and she took it out like it was a hot potato, almost scared to answer it. She pressed a button. She heard Justin's voice on the other end.

'I've been on a call to Anna. This information you've got, it's not that complicated. It details plans to attack the Monarch, and in the next few hours, later on today. I've passed the detail on. You've done well.'

'You said not that complicated?'

'No,' said Justin, 'but then again, ciphers don't always have to be complicated, don't have to be impossible to break. You've got a lot of different people operating in that group. These are final plans. Maybe they don't want them to be complicated. Maybe they need people to understand.'

'I saw him,' said Kirsten suddenly.

'Craig?'

'Lying asleep in a room with many other men. He really is with Gethsemane. He really is gone. At least I think he's gone.'

184

'He's gone,' said Justin. 'You can't trust anything he says now. You can't.'

'I know, I know. Look, I'll call Anna, see if she needs my help.'

'Tight squeeze to get down to London before then. She might send the jet up, I suppose. Okay, I'll need to get on to coordinating with her as well. You take care of yourself up there. Once this is done, we'll get after the ringleaders.'

'At least Craig isn't involved in going after the Monarch. He's up here. So many, all up here. How big is this organisation?'

Justin gave a silent response before closing down the call.

Kirsten dialled for Anna Hunt, and after waiting for a couple of minutes, she heard a familiar voice on the other end of the line.

'Good work,' said Anna. 'I'll be able to intercept them. The Monarch will be safe. It should be interesting, actually. We'll wait for them. We'll not go after them too quickly. Make sure we draw the full extent of them out. See if we can trace back who's brought them in, and where they've come from. Smash them for good, smash them properly.'

'They won't all be there,' said Kirsten. 'Craig won't be there. He's up north at the moment with the rest of them in that group.'

'He's gone,' said Anna. 'You have to stick by that. Question is whether we'll get Gethsemane. Will he come to lead the attack?'

'Who knows? Anyway, I'm going to see if I can get back on the trail. Maybe I'll watch the farmhouse.'

'No, come down to the Aviemore base,' said Anna. 'Godfrey's there. He'll want to congratulate you. In the Aviemore base, you can watch it all unfold. They have the cameras from everyone's point of view. You'll see them all getting taken down. Maybe you'll spot some of them; maybe seen them before. You deserve it. Once we break the spearhead, the rest will fall.'

'If indeed, that is the spearhead. There's an awful lot of them up in that farmhouse.'

'Trying to snatch defeat from the jaws of victory,' said Anna. 'You've broken through. You've done it. We won't kill them all, we'll hold a lot of them. We'll get the information out of them. Slowly and systematically destroy the organisation. Go down to the base, enjoy yourself for once, and be thankful Craig will be out of it. You might still get him back, or at least make sure he doesn't end up dead. I have to go; take care,' said Anna.

Kirsten closed down the call, and wondered what to do. She took a walk from the house, down a couple of streets, and into a nearby coffee shop. She picked up the phone there while she sat and drank, wondering if she should talk to Macleod about the situation, but how could she? This was spy stuff. She could never tell him the real things that were happening.

She could talk about feelings, but how could he understand? How could he really give her an authentic piece of advice? *The situation is too complicated, anyway,* she thought. She took more coffee, and then realised that sitting around moping wasn't doing her any good. Either go up to see the farmhouse or go down to the base.

Kirsten drove out past the farmhouse. She approached from several fields away, but could see no activity. Maybe they'd realised someone had been in. She thought she'd been careful, but after all, she had dangled the leg, claimed she was having sex in that room. Maybe afterwards, comments were passed. People had said things. Maybe they realised she hadn't. Maybe then, they'd all scarpered with the attack going ahead this afternoon on the Monarch.

They didn't know what she had got away with. She'd carefully placed the detail back in the bag, only taking photographs. She was also in the wrong room for having taken it. There was nothing left to do, though, except head for the Aviemore base.

Kirsten turned the car around and began driving down the A9 along a familiar road, which climbed up high. Through the summit at Slochd, before it came down towards Aviemore. She looked around her. She realised she loved the highlands, and one thing she didn't want to do was leave here.

In summer, this world would have been green, but now you saw the snow on top of the hills not quite coming down to the road yet. It hadn't got that cold. You can head out from here into the absolute wilderness. She loved passing by lochs, the rivers that run down alongside the road. Long stretches of road that tore off into the small villages. You could get easily lost, completely away from everything.

She pulled over for a moment and sat looking at a little loch off to the side of the road. It wouldn't have much of a name, if it had any. She saw sheep on the other side of it, grazing. Life in the Service was hectic. She'd seen enough killing to last her a lifetime. She'd had to despatch people.

Kirsten never liked the word killing. Killing sounded like there was no purpose to it. Dispatching people, removing obstacles on the path to freedom. No, that was too American. Keeping the peace.

Kirsten got out of the car and felt the icy wind on her. She'd have to start again. Move on after Craig. Maybe she'd find someone else outside the Service. That could work. Someone who didn't know her day to day. She could keep a lot of it private from him. Someone who could ease her mind about men again. She felt the chill and thought back to only a few nights ago. Would it leave her? She hoped it would leave her. It would be an obstacle to ever loving again.

She realised that as much as she loved Craig, seeing him had been the best thing for her. She tried, given everything, but he was wrapped up in this. Kirsten couldn't follow him. She couldn't take that anger.

Kirsten saw a car stop farther down from her. A man got out, seemingly stretching his legs. He was in a warm winter jumper. Something about him made her smile. He looked over at her and smiled back. He was trim in his own way. Certainly not fighting trim like Kirsten. He had a good shape, and a rather fine chin.

Kirsten imagined him talking gently. One of those men you could see holding a babe in his arms, nurturing the child. He would help you with the washing, would help you with looking after everything, and still look magnificent and not worn down. She laughed at herself and wondered why kids had suddenly come into it. What sort of mother would she be, given her background?

He started walking more towards her, smiling at her. She smiled back. Kirsten was about to say something when, out of the car, a woman emerged. She was holding a child. The man smiled at Kirsten, and lifted the cover of a bin, dropping some rubbish in.

'Lovely day, isn't it?'

'It's always lovely up here,' said Kirsten.

'No better place to bring the kids up,' he said. He gave a smile and turned back to the family in the car. Kirsten laughed at herself, thinking he might come over. Suddenly make a move, speaking to her after pulling into a lay-by.

Still, he had smiled at her. She would take that. He obviously appreciated her, even if he didn't know her. She appreciated him. Kirsten turned and got back into the car, pulled away, throwing a glance at the happy family. When she drove past him, something suddenly clicked in her head.

She wondered what was going on. She looked at the clock and the attack on the monarch should start soon. A detour out to the farmhouse had made her late to watch the start of it. Another half an hour she'd be there. She didn't really care, but something was bugging her.

As Kirsten approached Aviemore, no attack had happened. She would have had a notification on her phone. Somebody would have told her she was missing it. Clearly, there was nothing. Something hit her inside. A sudden chill, whipping through her. Had it all been too easy?

She had bugged Craig, and the bug had stayed on. The bug had stayed on. Even if they hadn't checked the bug straight away, at some point somebody would have found it. This was a spy organisation. This was a rogue intelligence group. They weren't dummies.

She'd infiltrated the base. She'd thought herself good, thought she understood how to do it, and she did. But really? That easily? No other notes left out. Just one. Why? Why was the final attack plan laid out like that for people at the far end of the country? They hadn't talked about the monarch. They were a Service, well, anti-Service organisation now.

Maybe they were the opposition, but they had signed up to protect the country. They may not have liked Godfrey. They might have thought Godfrey was bad for the place, but these people got into it for a love for their country because they understood what needed to be done. They weren't all rogues. Weren't all like the men who had come for her. They were going to—she stopped. Don't think about that. They weren't all like these men, were they? They distinctly weren't.

Kirsten drove through Aviemore to the other side of town because the base, like so many places up here, was just an old house. As she drove, she wondered about the cars in front and behind her. They seemed to go the same direction as her. Now she turned on to a minor road where there weren't many things down this way. Yes, there were a couple of farms. Then she saw several of the cars pull away.

She would turn shortly, turning in towards the farmhouse. The old-style barn, the supposed collapsed farmyard. She pulled the car up short, turned and looked at where the cars behind her had stopped. People were jumping out of them now, dressed in greens and browns, faces camouflaged. One stood up and had a rocket launcher on their shoulder.

Kirsten got out of the car, and she saw the first rocket fly towards the building. An enormous explosion took off half the roof on the left-hand side. There were cheers, and another rocket, followed by a third from somewhere else. Half of the building was down now. Godfrey was in there. Anyone that wasn't with Anna Hunt, anyone of a high-level, would be in there. *Of course*, thought Kirsten, *they want Godfrey. They damn well want Godfrey*.

Chapter 24

Kirsten took her handgun out and raced away from her own car, using the terrain to shield her from those attacking the farmhouse. She knew she made the right decision the moment a rocket launcher blew her car up. She could feel the heat from the explosion, the dirt showering her. If they were going for Godfrey, then she would make sure she got to him first. She would get Godfrey out.

Kirsten didn't have time to grab her phone, didn't have time to call Anna, and anyway, she was in London. She was at the diversion. Most of Godfrey's best operatives would be out in that field to take down the attack.

She crawled up to the top of the small hillock that was protecting her, and saw many from the other cars running towards the building. Kirsten took off towards the cars at first. Seeing a man with the rocket launcher, Kirsten dropped to one knee, paused for a moment, aimed, and fired, hitting him in the head. He dropped to the ground, but she was off again.

She threw herself flat as gunfire raked across over the top of her. She rolled to one side, then up to a knee and fired at someone standing with a machine gun. If she ran hard, she could get close because most of them had already started making their way to the building.

There were two more left. They looked like they were standing guard over the vehicles. She ran in behind one vehicle and then had the glass shot out by a man with a machine gun, who was looking after them. Kirsten edged away around the side of the vehicle, heard the tires go flat, and the side of it being ripped apart by machine gunfire.

She stood up once, checked his position, then a split second later stood up again and shot him in the head. The other turned, but in that moment, she tagged him on the shoulder. His gun now spraying bullets widely everywhere, a second shot from her tagged him in the head.

Kirsten ran up to the prone figures, placing a second bullet in each of their heads, and turned towards the building. Kirsten had one advantage now. She was approaching the building, and no one suspected they were going to get attacked from behind.

The first three people she shot didn't even see her coming, and she tagged them to the ground, but another one stopped at the door, using it as protection. Kirsten threw herself to the ground as gunfire raced over her head. She crawled forward slowly, realising that the terrain was rising slightly up towards the house so the person at the door wouldn't see her.

As she got closer, she suddenly sprang up and fired several times. The person there ducked inside twice, but the third time they poked their head out, Kirsten tagged them and ran straight for that door. As she hurdled the body that had fallen forward, somebody else appeared at the door. They were too close for guns to have mattered, and Kirsten nutted them straight to their forehead. They went backwards, their head cracking off the wall, and Kirsten planted her gun butt straight into them. As they fell, she tagged them and started running down the corridor.

She had been briefed about coming down to see Godfrey and knew that the main communications were underneath. There would be a shell below, one they could lock down if she could reach it.

She stopped suddenly, a body on the ground. It was one of her colleagues. She stepped over it quietly but got the impression someone was watching from the corridor. Further down was dark, incredibly dark.

Kirsten dropped and fired around ankle height. Somebody screamed, shots went off into the ceiling, and there was a brief luminescence. Kirsten saw a figure, saw the head near the ground, and shot. The gunfire stopped.

Kirsten didn't wait and charged on down. Someone came round the corner. Kirsten hit them with an elbow to the face. She grabbed their head as they bounced off the wall, snapping the neck.

There were cries of, 'Spread out, find him. He's got to be somewhere.' She saw the blown-up doors of the underground bunker as she followed down into the depths. Reaching the control room, she saw three figures. They were looking up at the ventilation. Kirsten didn't hesitate, all shots despatched within a couple of seconds.

Men lay dead on the ground, but there was no relish from Kirsten. She didn't enjoy this, but went into a mode where she made it happen. Moving herself to one side of the control room, she was out of view of the main entrance and the doors that had been blown apart. She started looking up above her.

They'd been checking up towards the ventilation. This part of the building was under the ground, so there had to be ventilation. Otherwise, you'd suffocate, you'd die. There needed to be an airflow, but it could be a tight airflow for all of that. Kirsten thought she saw something on the ceiling, something that looked slightly loose.

A man ran into the room, and Kirsten despatched him immediately, but there were shouts behind him. *Blast it*, she thought. She went to the doors, or at least the opening where the doors had been. Staying out of sight, in behind the wall, she listened for people approaching. Someone was approaching on the floor. She could hear them crawling ever so quietly.

She jerked her head out low, saw him, shot him, and moved back in. Maybe that would keep them there for a while. Then there was a charge. Kirsten put her head out, saw three of them coming, and shot the first one. The next one grabbed the shot man behind the shoulders, holding him as Kirsten fired off more shots.

The man burst in through the gap in the doors, dropping the dead body he was now holding while number three was running after him. Kirsten ignored the first one, caught the third one with an arm, pulling him back out of the way of the doors, and snapped his neck. As the second one turned around with a gun being pulled out of his holster, Kirsten threw a kick up into his face. It stunned him for a moment, and she shot him dead. She heard a cry to 'hold, no more charging down'. She turned, looking up at the ventilation on the slightly dislodged panel.

'Time to go,' she said. 'You need to get out.'

The panel suddenly fell down. Slowly, something was edging its way out. She saw a foot, and she wondered, would you be able to see that from the corridor? Kirsten doubted it because the panel was over on one side. She let the foot emerge, followed by another while she listened, wondering just how long they would wait, and she glanced back. Godfrey, in shirt and trousers and a smart pair of black shoes, had reached the floor. There was no one with him. He had clearly got up there on his own. Everyone else must be dead. They hadn't found him, but neither had they just blasted away. They intended to take him, to steal off with him.

'Miss Stewart,' he said, 'it is fantastic to see you.'

'What the hell? They got in here. Wasn't anyone watching the outside? Wasn't anyone—'

'I think the time for recriminations is over. I've contacted Anna. There's a helicopter coming. We need to get outside to the chopper.'

'There's only one way out,' she said. 'Are you able to run?' It was then she saw him hobble. He was slow in the extreme.

'Have we got any other weapons in here?' asked Kirsten. 'I'm going to be running low soon.'

'Doubtful,' he said. 'I don't have one myself.'

'No?'

'We could try to go the other way out.'

'What other way out?' said Kirsten. 'I didn't think there was another way out.'

'I suspect they'll have it covered, but it's tighter and much more twisting. The good news is they want me alive.'

'Lucky you. They want me dead,' said Kirsten.

'A wise move,' said Godfrey. He hobbled back away from her to the far side of the room. He pushed a button and the panel door slid back. 'This way out,' he said.

'Won't they be there? Won't they be coming that way?'

'They can't come. You can only open the interlocking doors on the way out. They might wait for us, but they can't come get us.'

Kirsten rolled across the entrance and came up on the other side. Several gunshots fired down into the control room, but she was now behind the wall, away from the corridor.

'Go,' she said.

'You need to go first. I can lock up behind us. I can shut these doors. It'll take them time to get through.'

Kirsten tore past them into the corridor ahead. She turned around and saw Godfrey closing the door behind her. He set some sort of lock on it. They were inside a metal shaft. It was barely her height, and he was right. It was tight, but it stepped up and slowly they climbed until they faced a small door.

He looked at it and whispered to her, 'They can't get through that. It's impregnable, but as soon as you open it, somebody could be there, but you'll be opening it in their face. Really tight. It's like a maze as you run through. Deliberate,' he said, 'so nobody can sit and pick anyone off. It's an exit, but it's a hard-fought exit. You'll have to go through people, but they won't be able to just see you coming. But you'll also have to get past each one of them.'

'You guys need to learn about mobile base transports. Something on the move, not stuck underground.' She put her gun away, reached down to the inside of her boot, and took out a knife. 'Lock it behind us when we go through. Follow me.'

Kirsten pressed a button, and the door flipped open. A man standing there lunged at her. He could only have been three feet from her, but Kirsten pinned his shoulders before he could reach her with his arms, and she drove the knife up into his gut. He doubled over and as he descended, she drew it across his throat, pushing him to the floor.

She climbed over him, and turned the corner. There was

another man, and she drove a knife into him. As she got past him, another knife came at her. She stepped to one side, caught the hand, pinned it to the wall with her own knife before reaching up and breaking a neck. She released her knife to let him drop to the floor.

'Do you think they've got a helicopter for us?' she asked.

Godfrey looked down at his watch. 'Given the timings, about another five minutes.'

Kirsten took a deep breath. 'There's nobody here at the moment. Why?'

'Because it takes time to find. They're not going to send all of their people down here straight away. They have to cover our options, to watch. Now that we've entered, they'll know. They'll start running towards this maze. You need to be quick.'

'Is it just one way out?'

'No, there'll be options ahead,' said Godfrey. 'Options to keep them guessing, just in case this very situation happened.'

Kirsten wondered what sort of mind came up with that, but she ignored her thoughts and drove through the maze this way and that way, listening. The lighting was dim, but you could see. Then she heard some heavy breathing. She turned a corner, surprised a man in front of her, slashed his neck, and dropped him to the floor.

'Move it,' she said. 'Godfrey, flaming hell, move it. I can hear them.'

'My leg is broken,' he said. 'I can't move quickly, and neither can you render help because of the narrowness of the corridors.'

He hissed this under his breath. Kirsten saw an option ahead of her and whispered left to Godfrey. She moved this way, that way. Kirsten met someone else, dispatched him, then went right when there was an option, then left again. She then found one more person in front of her, a woman this time. She caught Kirsten when she turned a corner, pushing Kirsten off the wall.

Her head bounced hard, but as the woman threw a punch, Kirsten ducked. The woman's hand connected with the wall, and she screamed, but Kirsten was already up into her, driving the knife to her gut. The woman doubled over. Kirsten bent and drove her to the ground, crashing into the floor, and then put a knife across her throat. She turned another corner and saw daylight.

'We're here,' she said. 'We're here, Godfrey.' There was a noise in the wind, and she realised there was a helicopter, but it was some distance off.

'Does it come and land? Where does it land?'

Godfrey reach down to his watch and pressed something. 'I've just sent it a beacon. They know where we are. It'll land shortly.'

'I'll give you cover,' said Kirsten.

She watched as the helicopter came in. It was going to settle ten metres from them. Kirsten stepped out, knelt on the ground, and watched the corner of the house. A man ran round as Godfrey was moving behind her. She shot him, then turned and looked the other way to see another man coming and shot him. Then she was back and forward until she turned and saw Godfrey in the helicopter. She went to run towards it, but it lifted off.

'You bastard,' she yelled and scanned the surrounding building quickly. She had to get out of here. She had to get away. The helicopter was turning to move behind the house, suffering from gunfire coming from another direction.

Kirsten saw an outbuilding, ran towards it, jumped and pulled herself onto the roof. Someone was shooting at her, but she couldn't wait. From that roof, she hauled herself up onto the bigger one, got herself up to where the chimney crested the top of the building.

The helicopter was now lifting, rolling past, and Kirsten heard gunfire rake across the roof. She took a couple of steps, put her foot up on the edge of the chimney, and pushed off, throwing herself as hard as she could from the edge of the building.

The helicopter flew past, and she flung her arms out desperately. She may survive the fall, but she wouldn't be in a fit state and she'd be prime target. Her hands hit the skids of the helicopter, sliding along until she threw an arm around the stanchion that held the skid.

Desperately, she wrapped her arms, but as the helicopter departed, it clipped some trees, her legs smacking off them. She twisted this way and that, and then her arms slipped. Kirsten was maybe now some fifty metres away from the house and felt her grip go.

She caught a tree on the way down, reaching out for branch after branch, slowing herself until she collided with the ground. It was a hard thud, but it was a lot softer thud than not having had her speed broken.

She roused herself almost immediately, out of breath. She sucked in whatever air she could, turned and ran away from the house. People were firing now, but the gunfire wasn't ripping through the surrounding trees. It was dispersed, wide. She put her head down and ran as hard as she could, disappearing off into the countryside. All she needed to do was evade them. Evade them, and not for long. They would retreat from the base, back to wherever they were hiding out now.

It took Kirsten the best part of three hours before she felt she could come into Aviemore. She made for a hotel, booked in under a false name, paying cash, and collapsed on a bed. She'd asked for a first aid kit and thanked them when they delivered it.

There were bumps and scrapes, the odd gouge, but she was safe. She collapsed back on the bed, and felt her eyes close. Godfrey would've left her. The bastard would've left her. Her eyes shut and Kirsten drifted off, still fully clothed, to sleep.

Chapter 25

Kirsten didn't return to her flat but remained at the hotel in Aviemore. She picked up a hire car the following morning before driving down the A9 to an important meeting. Anna Hunt had called, saying they had to get together. Godfrey wasn't sure what to do. With so many people in open rebellion, she wasn't sure what was left of the Service.

It had been attacked at the highest point. Godfrey only got out alive because of her, and then he turned and left her. This was Anna coming to her, not Godfrey. They knew he was a target. It'd be difficult to pick out, but they had been dumb. There was an arrogance in what they'd done, an arrogance that wasn't good. Maybe Craig had been blinding her. Maybe the emotions she'd felt. Was it the trauma from even before that, when she'd almost been—? Yes, she wouldn't say it.

Kirsten pulled the car off the main road and into the car park of the coffee stop along the A9. It was off to one side, away from the main road. When she got out of the car, she took a wander before entering. Slowly, she climbed the round steps up into the circular room at the top of the coffee stop, where she ordered a drink and then sat down outside. As soon as she'd done so, a woman also emerged out through the door onto the veranda and sat down opposite Kirsten.

'Godfrey sends his thanks,' said Anna Hunt. She was wearing a large, baggy blue jumper. Her hair was tied up into two bunches. She wore glasses, black and thick-rimmed, and she had blue jeans on. Anna looked like a mum and you wondered where her kids were. She certainly didn't look like the classy operator that the secret world knew.

'He left me. He damn well left me even when I hung onto the helicopter.'

'Godfrey was pissed at that,' said Anna. 'Could have brought them down, could have held them up. I told him it wasn't good for him to leave behind his saviour.

'Damn right it wasn't. If I hadn't grabbed that helicopter, I wasn't getting out of there alive. It was touch-and-go, really touch-and-go. Tell me one thing. How did we not see it coming?'

'Because they went for the big time, didn't they? The monarch. The monarch was never in trouble. Should have seen it. I should have seen it.'

'These people signed up to save the monarch. Their problem isn't with him, it isn't with the country, it's with Godfrey. Who the hell's Gethsemane?'

'Gethsemane?' she said. 'Where do you know Gethsemane from?'

'Craig said it. He was the one he talked about. Were you not told?'

'I was told that Craig was with the leader, but not Gethsemane.'

'Who is Gethsemane?' asked Kirsten. 'We need to know.'

'We do. I heard the name once. It was called out. A jibe.

A jibe at Godfrey, but I didn't react. I asked him. He said he didn't know what it was about.'

'But he's lying.'

'Yes, he's lying. And he was lying then, but I didn't need to know. It wasn't important to what we were doing.'

'Well, it's clearly important now. It's enough to bring down the Service.'

'Of course, it is,' said Anna.

'Where is he? Where is Godfrey? Go ask him.'

'Sip your coffee and tone it down. Be quieter. You don't know who's listening.'

Kirsten sat back. Anna was right. She was getting emotional. She needed to remain calm, needed to remain detached.

Anna said, 'Godfrey has gone.'

'Where?' asked Kirsten.

Anna pointed off the veranda out to the mountainside. It was purple, snow on top and dark. Everything brown, heading into autumn.

'He could be up there. He could be over the road on the other side. Godfrey could be in England. He could be in China. He could be damn well anywhere. The man's taken this so seriously. He's gone into ghost mode. No one knows where he is. No one will know where he is. He sent me orders, though.'

'That's nice of him. Hide and get everybody else to do the dirty work.'

'He's told me I'm to bring this group down and quickly.'

'Well, I'm out,' said Kirsten. 'Nearly cost me my life this time. And the arsehole couldn't even wait for me.'

'You're not out,' said Anna, 'because I say you're not. Kirsten, you want to sort this out. You still want to know what's turned

Craig. Well, you might put him to one side. You might turn around and say, "He's gone, he's changed", but you want to know what did it, you want to know why he's changed. Listen, you'll do that with me. You got into the Service to serve and we're going to serve. We're going to find out what's wrong.

'If the Service has ended, if it's brought down, the country is at risk. Do you know what it would take to build it back up? We need to cut away the cancer. Need to cure it. We need to solve what's wrong with it. I need you with me. I need someone I can trust. That's you. I need someone else I can trust. That's Justin, and that's it. The three of us are going to work together and find out what's wrong.'

'You don't order me to do stuff. I'm done. Out. I get paid and I walk. I don't like this job. It will get me killed.'

'We need to do this. Without this being solved, the country is at risk. Godfrey holds so many secrets. If he's not the right person for the Service, if he's what's turning it into this, then we need to sort it.'

'What, and even sort him?'

'Of course. Gethsemane,' said Anna. 'Mark Lamb. Craig. These are the lines of attack, the first being Gethsemane. We need to understand what's ripped us apart. You're with me.'

'You can't make me do it. I don't take orders.'

Anna Hunt put her hand forward on the table. 'Put your hand in mine a minute,' she said. Kirsten did so. 'You've known me all along. I'm hard. Good at what I do. I can keep a secret when I need to, but the only reason I've ever done anything here is for the country I serve. I am not loathe to hang on to someone who isn't doing their job. Godfrey isn't doing his job. I need to understand if he needs to be removed. I need to understand how to put this back together again.

'Understand, you have lost Craig and you're bitter and angry. I've lost Godfrey—don't know who or what he is. I would've stood by that man all my life. Taken a bullet for him, and now I don't even know who the hell he is. Come with me. Let me find out. Let me find out who Craig is. Find out who the hell Gethsemane is and what we're doing. Come with me and Justin, and when it's done, if you want out of this Service, walk.'

'Godfrey told me nobody ever walks away from the Service. Nobody ever truly leaves.'

'You will. You have my word, and if anyone comes after you, I'll sort them. In order to put that in place, I need a Service. One that is not beholden to men who cut it up for their own purposes. We will go in dark, and we will not come out until we understand what the corruption is.'

'Give me a moment,' said Kirsten.

She drank the rest of her coffee, walked down the circular stairs, and out of the cafe. She followed the path that led across and onto wooden walkways and further paths along the side of the mountain.

Her moment took over half an hour. She thought about Craig, thought about being able to leave him behind. She thought about Godfrey leaving her behind. About loyalty. She wondered what Macleod would do. What would he tell her?

She couldn't very well phone him up and ask him about this. He had been such a guiding influence, but these days, she couldn't speak to him about what she did, not even the slightest. They may even watch him. Craig knew he was an influence.

Macleod would say that justice needed to prevail. He would say they needed to know what was going wrong and to put it right. It wouldn't have been about whether it was his job. He would just get it done. Macleod would've told her to understand who she trusted, to go with those people, and to solve what was wrong.

Kirsten wondered what he would make of all this. Everything she'd done, the people she'd killed, the people she'd saved, and the country breathed again. That was when she was at her best, working to stop the innocent dying in London, the time on the train.

So many times, she'd fought hard. She needed to fight hard again. The country was always worth saving. Anna was right. If the Service went down, a part of the defence went. She knew what could sneak in.

She began her walk back. As she did so, she looked on either side of the path. She saw the onset of autumn, of winter, but she felt in terms of her career, she was in the winter of it. So very few people to trust. She walked back across the minor road that led into the cafe. She looked up and saw Anna Hunt sipping her coffee and watching her. Kirsten made her way up and walked through the cafe onto the veranda, and sat down opposite Anna.

'A wise man put me into this. He told you what I was like.'

'He did indeed, and he was right about you. You're made for this. You're good, incredibly good.'

'So incredibly good, I nearly got myself taken by a lot of men. This needs done, but we all need friends to do it. I'll go with you, Anna. I'll go with you, and we'll rectify this. We'll find out what's happening, and we'll deal with it. I'll do it because I've got you and I've got Justin, but I am not here under orders and neither is Justin. We go as the three of us and we do it. As a team, we'll decide what's right and what's wrong. You need to be able to live with that.'

Anna Hunt laughed. She looked off to the mountain and then back. 'What's so funny?' asked Kirsten.

'I was going to ask you to keep me under check. I was going to ask that you made sure that my motives were pure, that this was all about getting back because I've got Godfrey on my mind. See, I loved him, the two of us. We were close, incredibly close once. But I saw him change, and that's why I went looking for Craig for you.

'I understand a lot of how you feel, desperately hoping you can turn him back. Godfrey's more sheltered than Craig, much more hidden away. I couldn't be sure he changed, but now I know. We go together and we'll make our decisions together and I'll listen to the pair of you. I'll consult and we will get to the bottom of it,' said Anna. 'If somebody needs despatched, I'll do it, and I will give our king his Service back.'

Anna Hunt stood up and put her hand out across the table. Kirsten stood, came round the table, and gave Anna a hug.

'When I felt down at my lowest,' she whispered in Anna's ear, 'when those men had me on the floor, you came. I'm here with you. I'm here with Justin. Let's get to it.'

The pair broke off the embrace and turned without a word, and Kirsten walked over to the stairs. Anna called after her.

'I'll see you in a moment. Justin's down below.' Kirsten walked down the circular staircase, stepped out into the car park, and a car pulled up. The window on the driver's side rolled down and Justin Chivers smiled at her.

'Good, you're on board.'

'Did she just phone you?'

'No,' said Justin. 'I told her you'd come. She wasn't so sure, but I told her.'

'What's she doing up there now?' Kirsten watched Justin point, and Anna approached with three coffees on a small cardboard tray.

'We know you. You understand that.'

The two women got into the car, and Justin drove. 'Where first?' he asked Anna.

'Yes, where?' said Kirsten.

'If it's agreeable to you both,' said Anna, 'Gethsemane. The last time I heard that word, I was in Germany. We fly to Germany and we'll find out who Gethsemane is.'

Read on to discover the Patrick
Smythe series!

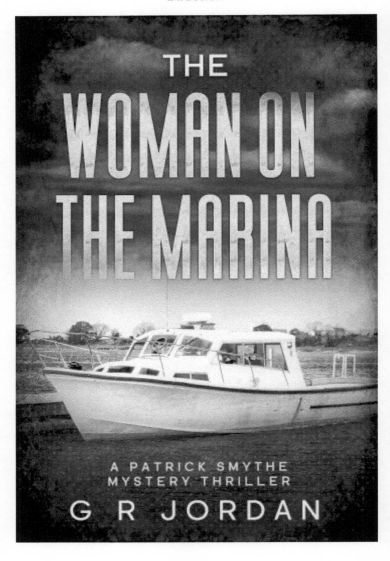

THE
WOMAN ON
THE MARINA

A PATRICK SMYTHE
MYSTERY THRILLER

G R JORDAN

Patrick Smythe is a former Northern Irish policeman who

after suffering an amputation after a bomb blast, takes to the sea between the west coast of Scotland and his homeland to ply his trade as a private investigator. Join Paddy as he tries to work to his own ethics while knowing how to bend the rules he once enforced. Working from his beloved motorboat 'Craigantlet', Paddy decides to rescue a drug mule in this short story from the pen of G R Jordan.

Join G R Jordan's monthly newsletter about forthcoming releases and special writings for his tribe of avid readers and then receive your free Patrick Smythe short story.

Go to https://bit.ly/PatrickSmythe for your Patrick Smythe journey to start!

About the Author

GR Jordan is a self-published author who finally decided at forty that in order to have an enjoyable lifestyle, his creative beast within would have to be unleashed. His books mirror that conflict in life where acts of decency contend with self-promotion, goodness stares in horror at evil, and kindness blindsides us when we at our worst. Corrupting our world with his parade of wondrous and horrific characters, he highlights everyday tensions with fresh eyes whilst taking his methodical, intelligent mainstays on a roller-coaster ride of dilemmas, all the while suffering the banter of their provocative sidekicks.

A graduate of Loughborough University where he masqueraded as a chemical engineer but ultimately played American football, Gary had worked at changing the shape of cereal flakes and pulled a pallet truck for a living. Watching vegetables freeze at -40'C was another career highlight and he was also one of the Scottish Highlands "blind" air traffic controllers.

These days he has graduated to answering a telephone to people in trouble before telephoning other people to sort it out.

Having flirted with most places in the UK, he is now based in the Isle of Lewis in Scotland where his free time is spent between raising a young family with his wife, writing, figuring out how to work a loom and caring for a small flock of chickens. Luckily, his writing is influenced by his varied work and life experience as the chickens have not been the poetical inspiration he had hoped for!

You can connect with me on:
- https://grjordan.com
- https://facebook.com/carpetlessleprechaun

Subscribe to my newsletter:
- https://bit.ly/PatrickSmythe

Also by G R Jordan

G R Jordan writes across multiple genres including crime, dark and action adventure fantasy, feel good fantasy, mystery thriller and horror fantasy. Below is a selection of his work. Whilst all books are available across online stores, signed copies are available at his personal shop.

Traitor (Kirsten Stewart Thrillers #12)
https://grjordan.com/product/traitor
An ex-lover at the heart of a countrywide take over. The Service fragmented and struggling to survive. Can Kirsten hold the country's spy network together and redeem her lover in the process!

When Craig is identified as one of the ringleaders in the attempted destruction of the Service, Kirsten struggles to believe it. Along with Anna Hunt, she must move quickly to quash the dangerous rebellion and prevent a national disaster. But can she pull her lover from the fire, or will he just be another figure to target?

Will love or loyalty rule the day?

Winter Slay Bells (Highlands & Islands Detective Book #29)
https://grjordan.com/product/winter-slay-bells
Sleigh bells ringing send a deadly warning. Christmas shopping becomes a matter of life and death. Can Macleod's team find the festive killer before the streets empty of Yuletide revellers?

The Christmas season becomes a season of dread and panic as a killer stalks the Inverness downtown shoppers during the busiest time of year for beleaguered local commerce. As the town prepares for a winter extravaganza Macleod must wheedle out the brutal murderer before the town is locked down and Christmas is cancelled.

Can you hear what I hear....?

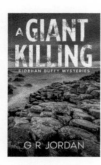

A Giant Killing: Siobhan Duffy Mysteries #1

https://grjordan.com/product/a-giant-killing

A body lies on the Giant's boot. Discord, as the master of secrets has been found. Can former spy Siobhan Duffy find the killer before they execute her former colleagues?

When retired operative Siobhan Duffy sees the killing of her former master in the paper, her unease sends her down a path of discovery and fear. Aided by her young housekeeper and scruff of a gardener, Siobhan begins a quest to discover the reason for her spy boss' death and unravels a can of worms today's masters would rather keep closed. But in a world of secrets, the difference between revenge and simple, if brutal, housekeeping becomes the hardest truth to know.

The past is a child who never leaves home!

Jac's Revenge (A Jack Moonshine Thriller #1)

https://grjordan.com/product/jacs-revenge

An unexpected hit makes Debbie a widow. The attention of her man's killer spawns a brutal yet classy alter ego. But how far can you play the game before it takes over your life?

All her life, Debbie Parlor lived in her man's shadow, knowing his work was never truly honest. She turned her head from news stories and rumours. But when he was disposed of for his smile to placate a rival crime lord, Jac Moonshine was born. And when Debbie is paid compensation for her loss like her car was written off, Jac decides that enough is enough.

Get on board with this tongue-in-cheek revenge thriller that will make you question how far you would go to avenge a loved one, and how much you would enjoy it!

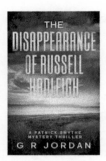

The Disappearance of Russell Hadleigh (Patrick Smythe Book 1)
https://grjordan.com/product/the-disappearance-of-russell-hadleigh
A retired judge fails to meet his golf partner. His wife calls for help while running a fantasy play ring. When Russians start co-opting into a fairly-traded clothing brand, can Paddy untangle the strands before the bodies start littering the golf course?

In his first full novel, Patrick Smythe, the single-armed former policeman, must infiltrate the golfing social scene to discover the fate of his client's husband. Assisted by a young starlet of the greens, Paddy tries to understand just who bears a grudge and who likes to play in the rough, culminating in a high stakes showdown where lives are hanging by the reaction of a moment. If you love pacey action, suspicious motives and devious characters, then Paddy Smythe operates amongst your kind of people.

Love is a matter of taste but money always demands more of its suitor.